Co-authored by Ann Frommer and Victor Merkel
TailGunner: War Defines Us
TailGunnerR3
TailGunner-Pip, Legacy of War

***

Also by Ann Frommer
Annie Cooks

***

Also by Victor Merkel
Misery Mountain
Constant Reminder
My Brain Aneurysm

TailGunner-Pip, Legacy of War

TailGunner-Pip, Legacy of War

Ann Frommer

Victor Merkel

Vicann Press

9310 W. Riverside Ave.

Phoenix, AZ 85353

First published by Vicann Press on December 3, 2017.

ISBN-13: 978-1981161607

ISBN-10: 1981161600

Photo by Donnie Serfass for Vicann Press

Dedication

To people everywhere, who were forced to make a living from laboring in coal mines.

My grandfather, Joseph Tumas, also had no choice, but to work in the mines of Pennsylvania. In Lithuania, he was university educated and from an upper class family. However, during the Russian occupation, he emigrated to the US. His immediate need was to provide food, clothing and shelter for his wife and five children. However, he lacked marketable skills and didn't speak English. The mines played a role in his early and untimely death.

Coalville, Coal Miners Hospital and Lansburg are fictitious and any resemblance to locations or facilities is coincidental.

Introduction

This novel, TailGunner-Pip, Legacy Of War, brings our readers to the third and final tale of Buck Remke, his son, Pip, and family. The gauntlet has been thrown down to a new generation. As a young adult, Pip accepts the challenge by going to Oxford, gaining new insight to his father's life, and faces head-on the struggles of becoming a doctor, choosing a mission and coping with romantic complications.

TailGunnerR3 finds Buck at home, a veteran, suffering from combat fatigue. Ilona's brother, István, fought the war in Eastern Europe but paid a heavy price for his loyalty. Pip grows up in a post-war world of love and hate.

TailGunner:War Defines Us follows Buck through high school, England, WWII and a love affair with cabaret singer, Ilona László. During the madness of war, a child is born. Ilona calls him Pip.

Acknowledgements

Ann Frommer thanks her husband, Robert, who has always given her encouragement without complaint. "He cheerfully consumed many meals of leftovers, allowing me to complete this trilogy."

Victor Merkel offers heart-felt thanks to Fran, his better-half for 20 plus years. "She kept me moving forward, offering her praise or criticism when needed."

"How can I take a final bow without expressing gratitude to the B-17 gunner's daughter, my niece, Leslie Merkel Kruize? She provided much needed insight while struggling to create the TailGunner Trilogy."

Special acknowledgement to Tom Cantillon who shared his expertise in character and plot development, plus correct language usage.

A huge 'thank you' to Yolanda Fundora for helping us create the graphics and colors for a professional book cover.

CONTENTS

CHAPTER 1: 1963 THE YEAR BEFORE GRADUATION, *OXFORD*

Closing his book and pacing in frustration. "Damn bloody mess! I'll never understand this formula, John, it makes no sense."

"Hang in there, Pip, chemistry isn't so difficult, it takes patience and understanding. Get it through that bloody head of yours to understand what's going on and what you want to accomplish. Patience, old chap, patience. How in the devil's name do you expect to become a physician if you fail a simple chemistry class? I mean, biochemistry...advanced. Stop your damn pacing, it's not getting you anywhere."

Pip stops, stands, furrows his brow, indicating his annoyance. "I suppose I expect everything to fall into place like my other courses. It's just *this* blinking one."

"You need to maintain a high grade for your scholarship funds, you know that," John lectured.

"It makes no sense, and I'm running out of patience. I've had enough of school, I really just need to clear my head."

"Pip, old boy, this is our last year. Remember our vow to stick together forever? To help each other out, no matter what we do or where we live?"

"Of course I do. We've come a long way, John, since we were twelve and thrown together into that blasted hell hole with that dreadful woman, Mrs. Savage. We worked our knickers off for the old bag, and still she abused us."

Putting the kettle on, John lamented, "I feel it's best to forget that part of our lives. Now, soon as this water boils, we'll be ready for tea."

"Right smart, John. Our whole lives are ahead of us. I will not disappoint you. Remember our late night stories at Wadsworth, when we planned our lives together? We promised to save humanity, help poor children, discover cures."

Pip returns to his books. "Let's start over on this bloody experiment."

CHAPTER 2: 1963 DANCE CLASS

"One, two, three, one, two, three, one, two, three. Loosen up man, loosen up. You're too stiff. Remember, you glide with the waltz, don't drag your body."

"I feel like a blooming idiot, dancing with another man," Pip admits.

"Why? A dad can't dance with his son?"

Struggling to stay in step to the music of "Moon River", Pip remarks while he stumbles about, "Sir, I've never danced before, never even considered it. Too many more serious things on my mind. Damn, I'm having a hell of a time convincing my feet to cooperate."

"Pip, relax, take it easy. Steps will come. Now tell me, why all of a sudden the interest in dance? Don't get me wrong, I would feel slighted if you asked someone else to teach you. You make me so proud, tops in your class at Oxford, prime member of the university soccer, I mean - football team and president of the debate team, asking your humble father, to teach you."

A blushing Pip explains the circumstances. "There's a ball. The Summer Ball is held each year. I don't go to such affairs, but this time, I have no choice. I was approached by the university principal that I will receive recognition for outstanding leadership. It covers a myriad of activities that I've been involved in."

"Sounds like a very prestigious honor."

"An honor, I am most unworthy of because John is the one. He's helped me with chemistry and his friendship has proven invaluable."

"How fortunate to have such a friend, but don't be so hard on yourself. Over the years, I've come to realize, I'm a pretty smart person and I deserve to have good things happen. I assume you will have a date, escort a young lady to this event?"

"Yes sir."

"Have you asked a young lady, as yet?"

"No sir," blushing.

"Anyone in mind?"

"Kind of," blushing deeper.

"Is she pretty?"

"Bloody yes. Excuse me...I, I."

"Don't apologize. How can I help?"

"Teach my feet to move in the proper directions."

"That's what I do. Now follow my lead."

Patiently, Buck holds his son tighter and whirls him around the dance floor until Pip relaxes and gives into the rhythm of the music.

CHAPTER 3: 1958 WADSWORTH SCHOOL FOR FATHERLESS AND MOTHERLESS BOYS

After the dance lesson, Pip returned to his room and reflected on a conversation he had concerning his relationship with his father.

It occurred while they were students at Wadsworth, soon after his father found him, he was annoyed because he finally adjusted to a new school with people who cared and an opportunity to attend university.

"John, I'm so bloody confused. My life was going right on until Buck showed up. I survived the Stepwell Orphanage, the foster home abuse of Mrs. Savage and now this."

"What is the problem old chap?"

"He wants to be part of my life, a life he never knew existed."

"No harm in that. I'd give anything to have my folks, even one of them back," he breaks down.

"Sorry, my friend, I did not mean to upset you. I came to realize that I was alone in this world and could manage on my own. Now this bloke comes along and wants to give me advice and tells me he cares."

"Damn right, it's a shocker, but must you fight it? Why not get to know the chap? Surely he's a descent sort of bloke. After all, he was one of our Allies, a tail gunner in a B-17 bomber."

"True, he fought in the war."

"And taken prisoner by the damn Nazis. How could you hate him because he loved your mum and their love created you?"

"I know, however, it still bothers me. Where was he when I needed him? I remember the elderly couple taking over for my mum. When they passed, I was thrown into a living hell at Stepwell Orphanage."

"Pip, it was the war, the system, not your father. He did not even know you existed. Appreciate that we're here at Wadsworth, other boys were placed in work houses or worse."

"Agreed, but he could have tried harder. I cannot forgive him for that. Damn bloody mess," Pip rants, ignoring John's reasoning.

"Get over it. He traveled across the pond to find you. Set himself up in a successful dance studio, he's here for the duration. Give him a chance!" John yelled, as he opened his books to study.

"Not easy, not bloody easy at all," Pip replies, sulking.

CHAPTER 4: 1964 FAMILY CRISIS

Buck quickly straightened up his modest flat, removed and folded the sheets and blanket covering the hide-away bed that doubled as a sofa. Dishes of uneaten food, the ruminants of his late night meal are removed from the narrow table in his small kitchenette.

Promptly washing dishware and cutlery and putting them away into his tiny cupboard, he inspects the small room so it's presentable for company. He fills the percolator with water, measures the coffee and turns on the switch of the two-burner hotplate.

Minutes later, a knock is heard on the door. "Hi Pip, come on in. Glad you could drop by on such short notice."

"Well, I sensed a note of foreboding in your voice. Not your normal self, Dad. Is everything okay?"

"You noticed? Well, first, let's head to the kitchen, grab a chair over here, next to the table. I'll pour some coffee. Would you prefer tea instead?"

"Coffee is good. You've spoiled me."

Moving one of the chairs from the sitting area, Buck sits next to Pip and leans into his son. "I...I have bad news Son. Your grandmother took ill late last night. Pop took her to Coalville Hospital. She was transferred to Allentown Medical Center. He sent a cable."

Pip's forehead wrinkled and his voice softened, "What happened to her?"

"The docs say Mom has heart problems. They're running tests now."

"Sorry, Dad. What can I do to help?"

Silence, lonely silence, while Buck stares across the small room.

"Well, I never wanted to think about this moment. You have your life and I have mine. Your mum is buried less than 15 miles from here, so I can visit her every Sunday. Up until today, life seemed...comfortable. Everything in its proper order. "An emotional Buck continued, "But now, I have to accept, my mother and father have entered their eighties and will not live forever. Since you're graduating from Oxford this week, now might be the time to visit your grandparents, before it's too late. I'll have to settle my affairs at the studio and prepare for the trip, soon as possible. Will you join me?"

After a few minutes of staring at his coffee cup, Pip replied, "Yes, of course, I'll go with you to the States...uh...Tamaqua."

Buck looked at Pip with relief in his eyes.

"My living arrangements will have to be settled and some debts paid off. However, I do need a break to determine my future," Pip reflected.

"Good." Buck nods his approval and clinks his cup against Pip's.

CHAPTER 5: 1964 OXFORD GRADUATION

After the graduation ceremonies, Pip and John meet back in their room. They opened the magnum of fine champaign, compliments of Buck and relaxed on the two chairs in their modest quarters.

Clinking their glasses together, "Congratulations, John. You've made top honors. I'm proud of you."

"Pip, old chap, your grades are right up there. You made top honors as well, your average was just a point below mine. It was a struggle but we did it."

"John, you've always been the smarter one. Things seem to come easier for you. They just don't for me."

"Chin up, we succeeded. The problem has always been obvious, you're too serious. Lighten up and reap the fruits of your hard labor."

"Easy for you to say, you have your life mapped out. My mind is cluttered. Not sure of my next move," Pip replied.

Pouring another serving of champagne, "Why not go on holiday, Pip? Our lives have been nonstop since Wadsworth, ten solid years of study, competitive sports and proving our worthiness of scholarships."

With a deep sigh, "My father invited me to go with him to the States. His mother is ill and the family sent for him," Pip directs his gaze to the activity outside. "He also suggested I take some time off from my heavy schedule to meet *his, er, my family.*"

"Seems like you're still not set on medicine. A break might be just what you need. This will give you the chance to clear your head and explore other opportunities. I hear they have coal mines in Tamaqua, Pennsylvania, maybe you'll become a miner."

"No thank you my cheeky friend, whoops, spilled some champagne on my shirt, but a trip away might be what I need. Perhaps the time together will give me an opportunity to appreciate my father better."

"What about medical school? We both have scholarships? They're not plentiful or easy to come by."

"If I still want to study medicine, I'll find a way, I always have," Pip answers, as he finishes buttoning his clean shirt."

CHAPTER 6: 1964 A DAY IN THE LIFE

The alarm clock buzzed without mercy.

"The start of another day, no, not just another day. Mom's sick and I, uh, Pip and I, must fly to the States," Buck says to himself while rising from his bed.

Bittersweet memories of Tamaqua High School, his old girlfriend, Laura, learning to fly at Arner's Airport and his caring parents float by as he prepares for the day. "My gray tweed suit, old school, yet assertive, will set the tone for changes I'll make today," he says, taking it from the closet.

Bam, bam, bam. A familiar noise rose from the floor. Old Mrs. Wallingford, in the flat below, smacked a broom against her ceiling to warn him when juvenile immigrants loitered outside.

"Mr. Remke, Mr. Remke, can ya hear me?" shouted Mrs. Wallingford.

These thin walls and floors are annoying at times.

"Yes, I hear you. How many?"

"Five, across the street. All Africans."

"Okay. I'll be right down."

Mrs. Wallingford asked Buck to act as the authority figure for this Stonebridge Estate building. Most of the renters grew up in London, survived the bombings in WWII and grew old through the 1950s, while Africans, Asians and undesirables from Ireland, Wales and Scotland flooded the city.

With anger, he slides on his suit coat, checks his shoulder harness and Colt .38 - backup in case things go to hell.

Grabbing one last sip of coffee, he takes the stairs down to Mrs. Wallingford's flat.

She grabs his hand and laments, "God bless ya, Mr. Remke. We've called the bobbies so often they won't come unless somebody gets hurt or dies. Those Africans can't just linger, threatening anyone who tries to pass. It's not right."

Buck smiles and tries to comfort her, "Don't worry, I'll talk to them. Warn the others to get their shotguns ready."

Stepping out to the sidewalk, he takes a deep breath and mentally prepares for the worst.

No, I've already experienced the worst, shot down over Germany and survived a Nazi death march. This, this isn't even close.

He checks his watch; almost 6:30 and as expected, the sun has risen over London about 15 minutes ago. Moist fog lifts from the city and the rasp of vehicle tires on neighborhood streets echo in the morning silence.

Local working people walking to the rail station, cross to the opposite side of the street. Away from the migrant bullies.

With his elbow pressed against the Colt .38, a supportive feeling, he makes eye contact with the Africans and walks straight across the street toward them.

Stopping at a close, yet comfortable distance, he picks out the leader.

"Good morning, gentlemen. Can I ask your business here?"

All eyes turn to him but no one speaks. They posture with an aggressive stance, angry faces and right hand near their hip. Street gangs were known to carry firearms in their belts.

Seconds later, one of them walks to the front and bellows, "Hey, wanker, you're not a bobby! Piss off."

"I'm sorry, my name isn't wanker, it's Buck. Who might you be?"

"Oh. Ya like ta play games, Mr. Buck? Knowing ma name won't help ya. The bobbies don't care, but...Zamir, ma name's Zamir."

The mouthy Zamir, looked young, but thin and hunched over in a James Dean type of way. His clothes hung loose, reminding Buck of the 'hand-me-downs' his brothers wore.

"You see the building behind me, Zamir? I speak for all 5 of those flats. Every one of them owns a shotgun and they have no tolerance when it comes to strangers lurking on the sidewalk. You need to move on."

"Ya blighter no longer own the streets. We outnumber your kind."

He reaches for his shirt and pulls it up. I see a large six-shooter, maybe Smith & Wesson, tucked under his belt.

"May be true, but if you pull that revolver, I will have to kill you. As for the rest of you, take a look at the windows. Each has a shotgun pointed at your heads."

Without taking his eyes off Zamir, Buck opens his suit coat and leans forward. His right hand reaches across and stops a few inches from the Colt.

Seconds tick by, anxiety increases, as Buck's fingers twitch.

Beads of sweat find their way down his forehead as he shouts, "Look, you don't want a blood-bath. Nobody needs to die over who owns this street-corner. Besides, you know the bobbies will hunt you down."

Zamir eyes him.

"How about, how about, I go to work and you get a free dance lesson. Free is good, right? I'm going to reach into my coat pocket and pull out a business card. Bring it to my studio and one of our pretty instructors will teach you the basics of Tango. Okay, Zamir?"

After hesitating, he takes the card, glances at it and then at Buck. The air stands silent between them. Buck thinks Zamir never received anything, unless strings came attached.

Without a word, Buck starts walking toward the station, never looking back. Turning the first corner, he steals a quick glance. Zamir must have decided to take my offer. Now, only woodpigeons dominated the sidewalk.

Leaving Aldbury Street, he sees Stonebridge Park Station in the distance. His pace increases as his mind turns to family. "So many things to do, how will I ever put my affairs in order?" He says to himself, his heart returning to a normal rate.

He pays at the gate and pushes into the crowd, lining up near south-bound tracks, headed for Kilburn High Road. Waiting within this sea of humanity, he reflects on his morning and his life.

No doubt, I live in a crime infested suburb, but Stonebridge Park also has the cheapest rent. Danger from muggers and killers? Sure, but I can't let it manipulate my plans, he thinks, glancing at faces around him.

My business has attracted some of the best dancers in London. Just another year and I'll move the studio to upscale West End, somewhere near Drury Lane. My primary concern now, can it survive without me for the next several weeks?

The sound of metal wheels on rails interrupts his thoughts. Glancing at his watch, right on time, the 7:18 pulls into the station. Like sheep, everyone follows each other onto the coaches.

Scanning the seats, Buck finds several open and sits near the door. Although the war has been over for 20 years, he still has a phobia about being trapped, whether in a B-17 bomber or a rail coach.

As the train starts rolling, he glances at his activity list. *Nigel, my number one man, prefers nurturing raw young talent. I hope he'll carry on as a teacher and 'manager' while I'm gone.*

Eleven minutes into his morning commute, the train slows to a stop at Kilbury High Street Station. Smells of oil, exhaust and blaring of a speaker, announcing their next run, permeated the air until he reached street level.

Only a few blocks ahead, walking north, past the retail stores and cafes, brings him to a red brick store front. Walterson Dance Studio, stands before him, a monument to all the long days, hard work and determination never to give up.

He walks into the reception area. Rachael and Nina, behind the reception desk, smile and wave, "Good Morning, Mr. Remke." They look busy, filling out forms and talking on the phone.

Without warning, Nina, the inquisitive one, jumps up and intercepts him.

"Mr. Remke, do you have a minute?"

"Sure, we can talk on the way to my office."

"Uh, okay. Well, I love it here, but when you hired me, we agreed on eight hours a day."

"Yes, I know. Nina, do you recall when I had this sales area built? Look at those shelves, full of dance trophies. The great talent we signed took place right here at these tables," he waves a hand, then looks at her.

"I remember. It seemed like madness at the time. I had just started and workmen flitted about with all sorts of building supplies."

"Well, back to your hours. Do you need time off?"

"No, nothing like that."

"Nina, don't mean to cut you short, but let's finish our chat in the lounge. Coffee? Tea?"

"Sure. Tea please. Never developed the taste for coffee."

"Did you know I designed this room to mimic the new discotheques?

"The lounge? No, I didn't."

"Yeah, metallic frames for the couches, plus lots of mirrors. Green and gold paint copies the latest hype from London, 'swinging city of the 1960s'."

"Mr. Remke, I admire how you've converted this place into a beautiful dance studio. You should be proud. Sir, about the hours."

"Yes, yes, of course."

Nina explained, "The walk-ins and calls from potential customers have increased, Rachael and I have been working almost twelve hours a day. We need another girl in the reception area, straight away."

Another reason why I can't run this place alone.

"Thanks for telling me, I'll hire someone, soon as possible. Maybe we can speed this up, do you know anyone qualified or who can be trained?"

"Hmm. Yes, I can recommend a friend, Mary. She has a public relations job at the Central School Of Drama, but wants to work in private service."

"Good, have her call me to set up an appointment."

"Thank you so much, Mr. Remke. You are 'top drawer'."

"Appreciate your confidence. Call your friend," Buck said.

Okay, let's see if I can keep my studio in the black for the rest of the day.

I'll try to sneak past the sales office - with all the inquiries, they don't need my help.

He heads to visit Emily, who keeps the whole damn place afloat. A few more steps and her office comes into view with a rectangle placard [ACCOUNTANT] mounted on the wall at eye level. He pokes his head inside and chortles, "Good morning, Emily."

She stares back, a semi-friendly, yet no-nonsense look on her face.

"No, not a good morning, Buck. Remember the discussion we had last month? Walterson's profit and loss, the figures haven't budged. You hired me to look out for your financial interests. We need to quit raiding the coffers for all this decorating."

"Emily, I respect your understanding of money, not everyone has a brand-new degree from London School of Economics. You have a way of dumbing down the numbers so even I can understand them. However, I must know how close to the flame this studio can fly without getting burned. We need risk-taking to attract the best instructors and students. Trust me, I've planned for some lean times, but we will weather this short transition period."

As the day comes to an end, he asks Nigel into his office, "So, Buck, what's on your mind that can't wait until Friday?"

"I have a problem, Nigel. My mother, back in the States, is suffering some serious health issues."

"So sorry, old chap. Anything I can do?"

"Yes, I think so. How long have we known each other, Nigel?"

"About two years, give or take."

"During that time, we've worked together through some lean years and you never let me down. I consider you, not only one of the best instructors, but dedicated to the survival of this studio," Buck says, looking Nigel in the eye.

"Buck, I'm flattered, but tell me true. Do you intend to sell the studio?"

"Not at all, Nigel. This studio has growing pains and with proper management will be ready for a move to Drury Lane by next year. The immediate problem is having someone assume management while I take care of my mother and beyond."

"You, you don't expect me...No, I'm a dance instructor, not a manager," Nigel shifts nervously and throws up his hands.

"Nigel, I'm running out of time. I need a manager tomorrow. I trust you, do you trust me?"

"Of course, but I only have a wee bit of experience. I might fail."

"We have a great staff that can guide you. Listen, this opportunity is for as long as you want. How does 30 percent of the studio sound? I provide financial backing and long range planning, you provide sweat equity."

Nigel puts a hand on his head, looking a little overwhelmed, "Oh my, in that case, you have a deal."

Buck rushes across his desk and they shake hands.

"You'll be fine. Believe me."

CHAPTER 7: 1964 ACROSS THE POND

"Pan Am, International Terminal, Sir," grated the cabbie.

"Okay, Pip, grab the bags, I'll pay the driver."

"On it, Dad."

I opened the rear door and stepped to the outside. The roar of jet engines overwhelmed me as I pulled a wad of pound notes from my pocket.

"How much?"

"Our standard rate, Sir," he says, pointing to the sign.

"Here, five pounds, keep the change."

"Thank you, Sir."

We entered the main gate into a massive open area loaded with signs, small shops and people, lots of them - walking, running, some wandering aimlessly, window shopping.

"This direction, Dad."

Pip seemed to know his way, so Buck followed him past the various gates.

"Have you been here before. Pip?"

"Yes, when I saw Uncle István off to Budapest."

They walked down a long corridor, until they arrived at their gate. Locating some seats near the ticket counter, they dumped their bags and tried to unwind until their flight was called.

"Pip."

"Yes, Dad."

"This flight across the pond makes me nervous. Doesn't make sense though, I crossed 22 years ago, from the States to England, in 1942, on a B-17 bomber and it didn't bother me," he paused, Pip looked at him.

"It'll be fine," Pip responds.

"Of course, memories of my last flight over Germany, in '44, gave me a lot of sleepless nights. Riding tail gunner position as usual, I took out a few Messerschmitts. In spite of my good day, those damn Nazis shot the plane out from underneath me."

Pip offered, "Well...Vietnam might be the only place we get shot down today."

"Amen, Son. Hey, you seem to be up on the latest with London Airport. Anything I don't know?"

"Well, London Airport is scheduled to be named Heathrow Airport sometime soon."

"So they'll name it after Heathrow, the small village nearby? Interesting. Uh...I hate to keep asking questions, but what type of plane will we board? Just curious."

Pip smiled, "I don't mind. We'll be flying on British Airways, Boeing 707. The newspapers say it has a good safety record."

"Good, I intend to catch up on much needed sleep. Last week had me dealing with some major problems at the studio. I've exhausted all my energy to make Walterson a solid organization so we can tend to Mom's needs without distractions."

"Attention all passengers on flight 843 bound for New York, JFK. We board in 20 minutes, please have your tickets ready," a voice spoke over the intercom.

"Okay, Dad, if you need to visit the loo, do it now, otherwise we might as well get in line for boarding."

"Good idea, be right back. Hopefully, I'll be good until New York."

"Dad, they have on-board toilets," Pip reassured him.

"It's not that. Just thinking about my studio. Hope it all goes smoothly while I'm away. I put everything into it," he says rubbing his hands nervously.

"Things will be fine, Dad."

Buck smiles, still looking somewhat anxious.

CHAPTER 8: 1964 ON BOARD

"Damn, passengers look stacked on top of each other, I just hope they pressurized this tin-can, unlike the B-17 bomber," Buck grumbles as they enter the plane.

"Dad, go about half way down the aisle, look for 22A and 22B. I'll follow you."

"Okay, son, but if you don't mind, I prefer the aisle seat."

"Fine by me, then you can have 22A."

They stowed their baggage and attempted to get comfortable for the flight. Pip started to read a magazine while Buck reviewed the latest edition of *London News*.

"Attention, please make sure you have safely stowed all luggage, trays and put your seat backs to its upright position. We will depart in several minutes," the stewardess projected over the loud speaker.

As Buck started to check the surroundings, a familiar sound triggered his awareness. Boots, heavy boots, shuffling behind, growing louder, unnoticed by the average person.

Two men, maybe late 20's, stop at the seats in front of them. He stares at them and a frothy, prickly feeling overwhelms him. Both wear military camouflage jackets and black berets sporting a round metal insignia, harp plus shamrocks, on the front. The word, 'volunteer', topped it off.

Although Buck didn't recognize the emblem, the shamrocks imply Irish origin. He knew the look on their faces, someone who has seen war. They glance about the cabin, evaluating everyone.

Buck whispered, "Pip, look at the two Irish soldiers about to sit in front us."

Pip looks up from his magazine and shrugs his shoulders. "What about them?"

"I don't know. Perhaps I've grown paranoid over the years. I'll be right back."

"Good morning, gentlemen. I'm Staff Sergeant Buck Remke of the 8th US Army Air Force, retired."

"Top of the morning to you, Sir."

"I wondered if you're Irish volunteers, traveling to join the US Army, 82nd Airborne on their way to Vietnam? The BBC recently had an announcement about it."

"Yes, we plan to join them at Fort Bragg, North Carolina for 6 weeks training and then off to Saigon," one of them remarks.

"I see. Well, good luck to you."

"Yes, and the same to you."

"Pip, I had a nice conversation with those soldiers. They'll join the fight in Vietnam," Buck says, returning to his seat.

"I know. I overheard you," Pip replied, still reading his magazine.

"Sorry, just anxious to get to New York. See my mom."

"No worries, Dad. We will be there soon," assures Pip, resting a hand on his dad's arm.

CHAPTER 9: 1964 WELCOME TO THE UNITED STATES

Pip remarked, "From what I can see through the window, New York goes on forever."

New York's always been an exciting place. My brief encounter occurred in 1943. After completing training in Nevada on .50 caliber machine guns and enjoying Xmas leave with family, I joined my crew members on our assigned B-17 bomber. Buck thought.

Pip was silent while he continued to stare out the window as New York loomed larger.

***

After landing, they followed the other passengers and headed for international arrivals.

"Pip, you'll have to enter the line for foreign citizens. I'll take the line for US citizens. See you on the other side."

"Okay, Dad."

"When we get back, we'll apply for dual citizenship."

"Sounds good. Then we'll both belong to the US and England."

Buck watched Pip walk to the foreign citizen line, then he rummaged through his bag for the passport. Dog eared and worn, he offered it to the attendant. He looked Buck over, stamped the passport and gave him a customs form.

The attendant pointed to baggage claim, straight ahead. Among the crowd, Buck found Pip waiting for their suitcases.

"Almost finished, Pip, after our luggage, we'll state 'nothing to declare' on these forms and arrange for a bus."

Bags in hand, they headed to the final check point. When Pip's turn came, he noticed the attendant appeared overly serious.

He looked at Pip and then his bag, "State your business here, sir."

"Visiting relatives in Pennsylvania."

"How long do you plan to stay?"

"I don't know. It depends."

The attendant gave Pip a cold stare and then nodded to an associate. He grabbed Pip's bag and pointed to a back room.

"You'll have to come with us, Sir."

As they started to walk away, Buck barked, "What's going on? You have my son there."

The attendant held up a hand and responded, "Stay back, Sir, and let us do our job."

The door closed behind them while Buck paced the floor. He wanted to kick the door down but realized that's a stupid idea.

Ten minutes later, the attendants and Pip emerged, his bag a mess and a blank look on his face, "You finished with my son?"

He responded, "Yes, welcome to the United States."

CHAPTER 10: 1964 BACK HOME IN PENNSYLVANIA

The next hour is filled with bus rides to Port of authority, then Tamaqua. Arriving in front of the Majestic Theater, Buck called the local cab company to pick them up.

He told the cabbie to stop at the bottom of Pop's driveway. The house looks smaller than he remembered and a huge pine tree dominates the front lawn. Memories wash through his brain as he recalled planting a small sapling there in his teen years.

"When I came home from the war, that tree stood up to my chest, now it looks at least 20 feet high. Nothing waited for me, the tree continued to get bigger and my parents grew older." With a lump in his throat, he waved the driver ahead.

"Dad, you okay? We can't sit here forever. I think someone just came to the front door," Pip said.

"What? Yeah, yeah. Your grandfather, most likely. Let's go."

They slid out of the taxi just in time to face Pop. Except, he no longer stood tall, like he used to. It appeared time has placed its hands upon him and bent him as he strains to stand upright.

Pop looked up with a strained smile and said, "Welcome home, Son."

"Glad to be home, Pop," Buck responded.

Buck's whole life, their relationship remained the same -- a firm handshake when arriving and leaving. This time he cast his mental taboos aside and hugged his fragile father. Pop seemed slightly annoyed but he didn't care.

"What about Mom? Have the docs been able to help her? We can leave at once to see her."

"No need to go right now, they did some tests, prescribed some medicine and she seems to feel better. The docs say she had a heart attack. Upset your mother a lot, me too. Thought she might die before you arrived. Tests and more tests. She needed a cardiac catherization so they transferred her to Allentown Medical Center. Coalville Hospital did not have the technology, "Pop explained.

Like a sudden jolt to the senses, Buck remembered Pip, standing behind him. "Pop, I'd like to introduce your grandson, Pip Remke."

Pip stepped forward and to Buck's surprise, Pop shook his hand and then gave him a long, emotional hug.

"I never expected to see you in this life. Your father struggled so hard to find you and in turn, we lost him to the quest. In spite of the odds, every day, your grandmother prayed for his success. She does the praying for this family since I have my own way of dealing with the world," Pop stated, as he shuffled about slowly.

"Well...Thanks for your good wishes," Pip strained, as his eyes watered.

For a brief, silent moment, Buck put his hand on Pop's shoulder and then on Pip's. Three generations of Remkes together in New England Valley. What a price he's paid to make this happen, moved to England, searched hundreds of leads, visited orphanages and nurtured a relationship once he found him. In spite of everything, this moment stands worthy of everything he sacrificed.

Wiping his eyes, Buck inquired, "Pop, we didn't get a chance to eat since leaving New York. You have any eggs and scrapple?"

"Sure Buck, with the chicken farmer just down the road, I always have eggs. As for scrapple, I'll check the freezer. Let's get out of the driveway before the neighbors start gossiping," Pop said turning toward the house.

Pip and his dad followed Pop to the kitchen. With two dozen eggs in the fridge and a pound of scrapple in the freezer, they all pitched in. Pop fried scrapple while Buck tackled the eggs. Pip set up the percolator and brewed a fresh pot of coffee.

With a plentiful setting of food on the table, Pop announced, "Okay, boys, let's eat."

Buck responded, "Thanks Pop, it looks great. If you don't mind, I need to say a few words on Mom's behalf."

"Sure Son, if it puts your mind at ease."

"Okay, here goes. Dear Lord, the Remkes have always been a tough breed. As a family, I know we'll come together for Mom. I also pray the doctors will find out what ails her and fix it. Thank you. Amen. Now...we can dig in."

CHAPTER 11: 1964 BLAST FROM THE PAST

Buck and Pip eventually ran out of supplies, and drove to Wanamaker's Grocery in Tamaqua for food, laundry soap, and other random items. As they checked the aisles, a middle aged woman walked toward them, but she looked busy perusing the cleaning products.

Buck looked at her, remembering…*I know this woman, perhaps too well. In 1939, twenty five years ago, Laura and I dated in high school, talked about marriage and shared each other on Tuscarora back roads.*

It didn't end well. While I went off to war, she married a 4F, someone not fit for service. A classmate with no patriotic qualities whatsoever.

In 1945, when I returned as a war hero, Laura and her husband Reggie happened to meet me by chance at the East End Fire Company bar on a Saturday night.

***

Loud country music filled the air from a three piece band while couples danced on the crowded floor.

Laura smiled at me and uttered some bland non-sense about wishing me health and happiness since I returned. No apology from Laura for screwing me over with a failure like Reggie.

I grabbed her arm and vented, "You didn't wait for me. Why?"

Reggie interrupted, "Son of a bitch, Remke! Keep your hands off Laura, before I get pissed."

"Oh yeah. We went together long before you, Reggie. I've touched a lot more places than her arm."

"Well...you got the short end of the stick, Remke. She belongs to me now."

I stared at Reggie and then at Laura. I chuckled, "You sure."

Reggie's face turned red and he waved a fist at me.

"God damn you, playing the big brave man, back from the war. I bet you never saw action, just sipped tea with the whores in London. In fact, it all makes sense now, a half Jew whore spit out your half Jew son."

That's all I needed, so I grabbed Reggie's shirt collar and pushed him against the wall.

"You and I need to take a walk out back, you crazy bastard. We'll settle this once and for all."

"You got it," Reggie boasted.

Reggie was a complete fool to accept the challenge. During the war, I trained in martial arts and survived a Nazi death march. Both gave me the skills and attitude to disable or kill an adversary, if needed.

Soon as we reached the alley, Laura and numerous gawkers stayed at the back door. I walked near the center of the roadway and sized up my adversary. Reggie circled me, acting like he had an advantage.

Reggie also moved his arms about in bare knuckles fashion, like the 1880's champion, John L. Sullivan. I imagined, he didn't know, street fighting fell short when compared to Asian based martial arts.

I challenged him, "Look, Reggie, this is your only chance to apologize. I'm fed up with you. First, you stole my girl, while I fought in Europe. Then you slandered me and my son. Apologize now or I will kick your ass."

"Go to hell, Remke."

I realized our discussions had come to an end when he squared off. Reggie took numerous swings which I dodged, bided my time, waited for an opening. Soon enough, with a short jab, I broke his nose.

The rest seemed like a child's sand box scrap. Instead of fighting, Reggie tackled me and managed to take a few swings, which I blocked. At close range, I jabbed just below his rib cage, leaving him gasping for air.

Looking down on Reggie, I saw a fat, Jew-hating man, soured on life. He managed to get up and started fighting again, but I wanted to end it. I swung a hard right to his jaw and sent him face-down in some raw sewage. He stayed down and I never saw them again.

***

Interrupting his thoughts, Buck approached the woman, "Good morning, Laura."

She stopped and stared at him for a moment.

"Buck? My god, I never expected to see you again. What brings you to Tamaqua after all these years?"

"My mother had a heart attack, she's up at Allentown Medical Center. I'm here to help, any way possible. I'll stay until she recovers."

"Sorry to hear about her. She always treated me with kindness."

"Thanks for your concern, Laura. Geez, I remember, we didn't part on the best of terms, I'm sorry about that. Afterward, I just wanted to forget about the fight. Can I ask about your husband, Reggie?"

"Oh, I divorced the bastard. I knew he had a temper when we married but he never hurt me. Then one day when the local dairy fired him after 17 years, he went crazy, broke my jaw and punched me in the face until I blacked out. They put him in prison and I filed for divorce."

"Sorry, but I'm glad you're done with him. What about now, any special man in your life? You still living in New England Valley?"

"No one in particular. I moved to Tamaqua, on Orwigsburg Street. If you have time, drop by, maybe we can split a bottle of wine. Talk about old times."

"Uh...my son, Pip, joined me on this trip. Hmm, where did he go? Well...anyway, maybe, if I have time."

Laura reached in her purse and pulled out a card.

"I have Sunday open, Buck. Call me if you can make it."

Laura sauntered up to the checkout, while he watched her. She lost weight, accentuating her best features and seemed more mature than when he saw her last.

Buck then wandered the aisles until he found Pip in the food aisle. He had loaded the cart with canned soup, beans, bread and 2 pounds of sliced bologna.

"I wondered where you roamed off to while I talked with my old classmate, Laura. You didn't have to leave."

"Dad, I'll turn 21 this year and lived long enough to know when two people share a history. She seems like a nice person. Did she ask you to visit?"

"Buck hesitated and then sighed."

Pip jumped in, "Smashing, then, no harm, no foul. I can't see Mum wanting you to be alone for the rest of your life."

"I know, Pip, but I also have Mary, back in London, to think about. I can never be more than a friend to Laura."

"Then go as a friend and catch up. Have a good time."

"Maybe, Son, maybe," he responded, as they headed to the register.

CHAPTER 12: 1964 OLD HAUNTS

"Pop, do you want to drop by the vet's group? I plan to see if any of the old crew still go there."

"No thanks, Buck. Most of the WWI vets I know died off and the rest just don't go there anymore. They don't want to show up in a wheel chair, crutches or as a shuffling old geezer. General McArthur said: 'old soldiers never die, they just fade away'. He sure as hell meant every word."

"Well...I'll let everyone know, you walk on your own two feet and live an independent life. It's sad when old soldiers like you, Pop, can't come together and feel good about it. I still remember the old pictures of you in uniform, standing tall and proud. You served, and this town owes you. If the local groups won't meet the needs of WWI vets, then I will find a way.

Pop reflected, "Come to think of it, I sure miss a spirited game of poker with my old buddies. Oh, I enjoyed the game with you, Buck, but those guys like to play high stakes, even if just for pennies, and bluff the pants off a buffalo."

"I'll keep my eyes open, Pop, I still know a few class-mates in town, well-heeled, thanks to their parents, but do the mercenary bastards even care about vets? Far as I know, none of them ever served in the war. I'll start talking to people right away."

Pip interrupted, "Ready to go Dad? I've never been to an American pub."

"In the States, they call it a bar, although I heard some Brits opened a pub in Philly. No matter the name, most sell beer and liquor. The place we'll go to first, the vet's group, downtown. They honor veterans who fought in wars overseas. They have a bar and tables where vets can associate with fellow vets."

"You've piqued my curiosity, Dad, where else do you plan to go?"

"The second place, East End Fire Company, will be more to your liking, young people in the 21 to 35 crowd. I doubt if many forty one year olds, like me, still go there. They will, most likely, still have fast music and dancing. In the fall of '45, I spent a lot of time there, looking for relief, from the flash backs, in a bottle of beer. When I came back from the war, I found out what combat fatigue means. In my head, I remembered all the horrors of world war two -- planes crashing, men dying, loud explosions plus the brutality of Nazi guards in my POW compound. Still do, even today."

Pop counseled, "Pip, you never want to forget what your father went through. He survived it, and in a way, made this family stronger. Makes us grateful for our freedom."

"Dad...do we need to go there? If it represents such a hurtful part of your life, we can stay at the vet's group or come home."

"No, Son. It represents more than a tavern where I languished for several years. The East End also served as the site where I thrashed a racist bastard, called Reggie, and defended your honor. Pip, it stands for part of your American heritage. Years from now, you can tell your children, 'Grampa not only survived the war, but kicked combat fatigue and moved to England.'"

"You boys had better leave if you hanker to catch supper at the East End," Pop advised, "You plan to eat there, don't you?"

Pip chimed in, "Grampa's right, we don't want to be late for our dinner, er supper."

"I know. So much to say and do, but not a lot of time. Tomorrow we visit your grandmother. We can get an update from the doc. Then, she can tell you about her life and raising a family in the valley."

CHAPTER 13: 1964 TUMAS CAFÉ

"Dad, the phone has been ringing off the hook since we arrived in Tamaqua. Seems like you're some kind of hometown hero."

"I'm surprised too. It's just the guys I went to school with and some of the others, who are friends of theirs. They heard I was home, so the gang wants to meet at Tumas Café to catch up."

"News travels fast around this home town of yours. I'm curious. Mind if I tag along?"

"Of course not. This hasty reunion gives me the chance to introduce you to the men I grew up with. Also, you'll have a face to go with the stories about them."

"Is it okay to leave Gram? She came home from the hospital, only two days ago."

"I think so. Mom is resting quietly in her bedroom. Pop is here in case she needs anything. Mrs. Baker, the neighbor down the road, brought one of her famous casseroles and all they have to do is heat it in the oven."

"Good show, Dad. I have been looking forward to visiting Tumas Café...meeting your old chums."

They borrowed Pop's pickup truck and drove into town. Buck pointed out some of the places he frequented in his youth.

"We're on Spruce Street, now to weave our way to Tamaqua High School. Look…see the main steps. Our gang used to hang out there at lunch and toss a soft spongy ball for entertainment. Listen to this, one of the guys threw it too hard and accidentally hit Principal Skinner on the head. Although the only thing damaged was his dignity, he put six of us on detention with a note to our parents."

"Ha, ha, ha, ha! You in detention. I'd give a hundred pounds to see you in those straits. You know, Dad, except for the sad reason we had to take this trip, I am happy to spend time with you, meet the family and see where you grew up.

"However, doubt if I could ever master driving on the right side of the road in the U.S. It's quite unnatural," Pip exclaims.

"I felt the same when I came to England and still have to remind myself it's correct. However, those rotaries just frustrate me to no end."

"After all this time you're still not used to the *roundabouts*, Dad? I guess your American values are hard to compromise. Take your beer, you like it cold, I'm partial to room temperature."

"Yeah, I'm working on it. Give me another ten years."

"Okay, now we'll head over to Tumas Café. It's only a few blocks from here."

Buck bobbed and weaved down side streets, then pulled up to the curb.

"The café's right there, on the corner."

"Reminds me of the pubs back home."

"Yes, I imagine, back in the day, England influenced a lot of construction in Pennsylvania.

"Regarding the café, Mr. Tumas serves food, besides tending bar and his wife cooks. They live above the café. Now you know a little about them, so let's go in," Buck says, parking the car.

Upon arrival, they see Joe Tumas, a silver-haired man, smiling and filling two beer glasses from the tap.

"Have seat gentlemen. Good to see you again, Buck. Put your money away, my treat, for your service during the war."

Buck modestly takes the two glasses and gives one to Pip. "Thanks, Mr. Tumas." Looking down the bar, he sees familiar faces of men who are parked on the stools.

"Hi, Buck. Welcome home. Been a while since you've been back."

"Hey, Phil. Maybe too long. Glad to see you're still alive. We both had a rough patch with combat fatigue back in '45. Oh, by the way, this is my son, Pip."

"Handsome bugger. Has your dimples, Buck," Phil says, raising a bottle of Yuengling beer.

Blushing, "How do you do sir?"

"Where'd ya get that accent? I forget, yer a limey, aintcha?"

"Sir?"

"What Phil means, son, is that you're British. Take no offense."

Pip smiles and extends a hand. "My dad told me all about you and the other chaps. Pleasure to meet you."

"Hey Buck, he's all right. Let me introduce you to the rest of the Tamaqua gang. Scuse us, Buck."

Buck chatted away with the men. Guys from high school sports and some who played in the school band. As he sat and talked, more fellows came over to shake his hand and welcome him back. The conversation continued back and forth about each other's lives.

Later, Mr. Tumas announced, his wife had fresh split pea and ham soup ready to serve and the Italian baker just dropped off rolls, hot from the oven.

The men placed their orders and moved to the small restaurant up stairs. They sat around two large tables and ordered a round of draft beer.

Questions and answers are interrupted by slurps of fresh hot soup, chomps of warm Italian rolls and chugs of cold beer, until one of the men opened up that they needed more activities and outlets after work.

Buck was surprised by this frank admission and he pressed for more information.

"What would you like to do? Do you have any idea? What do your wives like to do?"

"Don't know? The wives usually mind the grand kids. Otherwise, they play some Canasta, Bingo or attend Rosary Society. As for us, we're tired after a hard day at work and don't want to do nothin," Bobby lamented, "Ain't good for us, I'm told."

"Really? You must do something!" Buck inquired.

Bobby groused. "Eat supper. Have a beer, here with the guys. Poker game once a week. Watch TV."

Buck sympathized. "Same old routine, it seems."

"Yeah," Bobby groaned.

"What about some sort of exercise or other physical activity?" Buck questioned.

"Buck, you must be shittin us. Sammy over there, he works in construction. Mikey works at the Atlas, he's up on telephone poles and ladders fixin the damn broken electrical units. Then there's Phil, he got himself cleaned up, now he drives a truck for Eames Bakery. I'm a plumber. Crawl on my hands and knees fixin shitty toilets and leaky pipes. Many of us worked in the mines until other jobs came up, our damn coughs give us away. We don't need no more exercise. Geez."

Bobby looks at the other guys, who nod in agreement, then he takes a swallow of beer and places it on the bar.

"What I'm trying to say, some activities can energize and tone your body so you'll feel better afterwards."

"Buck, I don't want nothing to do with 'pep' pills. The VA docs prescribed them after the war when we were havin some 'adjustment issues', as he called it. Some of us got hooked. Took a long time to break the addiction and take ourselves off em," Bobby said, defensively.

"I'm thinking of something else. Something you can do with your wives as well."

"Well...some of us want to get away from our old ladies. We like to spend time with the guys after work."

"Okay, with or without your wives. When did you guys last dance?"

"Dance?...You must be out of your mind. I ain't gonna do no dancing!" Bobby shouted.

"I used to be like you. After the war, the combat fatigue took over, I had no focus and couldn't get my head together. Arthur Murray opened a dance studio in Allentown and offered a few free lessons. For whatever reason, I walked into the studio and they changed my life," Buck admitted.

Now, just hear me out, guys. The dance instructor, an attractive woman, knew what I needed. She convinced me that I could tango. Consumed by the challenge, I allowed the music to enter my body, made it move with the tempo of the music. My experience with dance was better than any medicine. I'm telling you the truth."

"Wait, you just walked in from the street and let this dame lead you around on the floor? Didn't you feel like a jack ass?"

"I was self conscious at first, but 'Lottie', directed my body to move with hers. We were like magnets."

"Hey, you said she was attractive, but was she sexy?" Bobby questioned.

"I guess she might be called sexy. More important, she was in terrific shape. Dancing is a great workout. Keeps you young," Buck said, looking at the faces around him, in their disbelief.

Phil piped up, "Hey guys, listen to what Buck has to say. He saved my life more than once. My mom still prays to St Ann for him every morning, she is so grateful."

"Is that so, Dad? What kind of miracle did you perform?"

"Not much, no more than any friend would do to help another, Son. Phil is also a vet like me. In fact, all of these guys are vets. We answered the call of Uncle Sam to serve our country."

"Yeah," Phil interrupted. "Buck here is famous, in case you don't know. He sent me pictures of his dance place in England. In fact, I have a newspaper clipping. He's made it big over there. You should listen to im."

Buck went on, telling them stories of his mission to find Pip and the good fortune with Walterson dance studios. Pip observed the vets listening and hanging on to every word. In between the questions, he heard frequent deep coughs.

"Tell ya what, I'm bringing Pip to Dr. Bartulas' combat fatigue support group at St. Ignatius Lithuanian Church tomorrow evening. If they can spare an empty room and a phonograph, I'd be happy to demonstrate a few steps and work with you then. If you want, that is," Buck said, nursing his beer.

Pip observed the reactions amongst the men. Poking each other, some appeared to think it was humorous, others listened with interest. A few seemed like they might take him up on his offer.

CHAPTER 14: 1964 MIKE

Pip bathed in the strong bond of Buck's family. Not like that disappointing weekend, when he was a Stepwell orphan and the seemingly loving couple selected him to come to their exquisite home. They dressed, fed and indulged him, until the missus felt Pip reminded her of their dead son, he found himself returned to the orphanage.

These people right here, in this small town, and my family, are truly upstanding. Also, the guys have such high respect for Buck. I feel closer to my dad now.

"Dad, think Grampa would mind if I take the pickup to town?"

"Probably not. You can ask him when we get home."

"I will. I'd like to drive around and explore the area more. I might even stop at Tumas Pub, er Café."

***

"The steering wanders a little but otherwise this old '50 Chevy 3100 truck runs fine. Oh, one last thing, remember to drive on the right," Pop mentored.

"Got you, I won't forget. I promise," Pip said.

"Good. Now, before you leave, do you have any change?" Pop asked.

"Change?" Pip questioned.

"I mean US quarters, dimes, nickels."

"No, no I don't, Grampa, just dollars."

Pop reached into his pocket, pulled out some coins and advised, "Tamaqua has parking meters all over downtown. Here, five nickels should give you plenty of time to see the sights."

Pip drove into the small town of Tamaqua. He took note of the train tracks that ran north and south through the center of the town. Pulling up to the station parking meters, he reached into his pocket for the nickels his grandfather gave him.

I'm glad Grampa warned me about the police giving tickets if they're empty."

Finding a bench in front of the train station, he relaxed, taking in the hilly landscape on the horizon and cars going through the downtown, 5-points, intersection. Soon after, an old timer hobbled up to the long wooden seat and parked himself down beside Pip.

"New in town? I ain't seen ya around before. Name's Mike,"he said, extending a hand.

"How do you do, Mike. I'm Pip. I'm here with my dad. We're staying with my grandparents."

"Ain't that nice (cough, cough). Ya don't sound like yer from these parts," Mike struggled to say.

"No, sir. I live overseas. My dad as well."

After a few rounds of small talk, curious, Pip asks, "What kind of work did you do Mike, if you don't mind my asking?"

"Hell no, Son. I was a coal miner. For more years than I'd like to remember (cough, cough). Been retired ten years. Small pension and social security just about cover me, the wife and expenses.

"See them tracks? Four railroad companies owned trains that traveled those rails. The coal was mined, piled into coal cars and transported to different parts of the country, hell, to different parts of the world even (cough, cough). Excuse me, I can't stop this blasted coughing, the damn mines did it to me."

"Can I get you a drink of water?"

"No thanks, Son, the cough has to go its course."

"Is there any cure? Relief for your cough."

"Fraid not. It's common amongst miners due to the coal dust. The damn doctors don't care. They got tired of seein us," he admitted, coughing more. "Sure, there's a clinic, but the doc just handed out sugar coated pills, gave us vile tasting liquid and told us to take deep breaths."

"So sorry to hear that Mike, I suppose a lot more people suffer with the same kind of cough, here in town."

"Too many, Son."

After chatting a little more, Mike looked at his watch and said, "Hafta go, the missus will be lookin for me. Probably has supper on the table. Nice talking to ya."

"You too, Sir."

Pip watched Mike drag his feet as he headed to Broad street. "Crying shame. Works his whole life and what's he left with, a damned cough and not much else. Someone must be able to help him," Pip uttered to himself.

CHAPTER 15: 1964 PIP AND GRAM

Pip awakes from his sleep in the Remke attic. The attic that held beds for the four Remke brothers. He remembers the stories his father told, about the pillow fights and ghost stories to scare the younger boys.

The aroma of fresh perked coffee, bacon, eggs and toast permeates the air, urging him to rise.

"Hey, sleepyhead, breakfast is on the table," Gram chuckled, as Pip entered the kitchen.

He was surprised to see his grandmother dishing out portions of breakfast onto his plate.

"Gram, are you supposed to be up and cooking breakfast?"

"Dear, I feel fine. That bed was beginning to wear on me. I feel better when I can work around the house and garden.

"I wanted to thank you for coming to the US with your father. You boys visited every day while I recovered at Allentown Hospital. Our little talks about family helped me to forget my heart problem and I hope, gave a sense of where you came from."

Pip nodded, "I will always be grateful for our talks."

The small, smiling woman proceeded to pop another slice of rye bread into the toaster after she buttered the one on his plate. "I'm so happy you're here, Pip. At my age, I didn't know if we would ever meet."

He walked over and gave her a hug, "Thank you. I'm so glad we came."

Pip feels at home in the comfort of the Remke kitchen. Meanwhile he thinks about what his mum's family kitchen would have been like, as he bites into the toast.

That will be a topic of conversation when Uncle István and I get together.

CHAPTER 16: 1964 ST. IGNATIUS LITHUANIAN CHURCH

Arriving at St. Ignatius Church for the veteran's support group, Pip recognized some of the men from the Tumas Café group. The group welcomed him and introduced Buck and Pip to the new guys. After coffee, tea and soft drinks had been served, the men candidly spoke about their lives, the hurdles and small successes they achieved.

Dr. Bartulas, the group leader used a different tactic than when Buck was a member of the group. Instead of listening, he gave directions to the men, such as…"You say, you cannot find a job. What have you done so far? Or, you say you are bored, what have you done about it?"

He was aware of Buck's success with his dance studio. In a previous conversation with Buck, he had arranged for one of the rooms in the church to be available for dance lessons. Dr. Bartulas shifted the conversation about the benefit of dance and planned to join the group. "Men, some of us, me included, can stand to lose a few pounds. The dancing will help."

"Buck made the men stand in a line, follow his steps and feel the rhythm. Some followed and seemed to have a good time. Buck remembered them as the best dancers in high school. They were always the leaders so he knew the more timid would follow. Pip, watched for a while, then left the room for a bit.

When Pip moved to the outer room, he saw a man standing there watching. Pip smiled and directed him to the room where the activity was occurring.

Of course, when he spoke, Pip's accent sounded unlike one who was born in the US. The stranger took issue with his accent.

"Who are you?" the man asked, eying Pip.

"Sir? My name's Istvan Remke, they call me Pip."

"You're the little Jew, huh? The bastard child from Buck Remke and a Hungarian slut."

Pip's face reddened and voice hardened, as he responded, "I don't know your problem, but there's no need to be rude."

The stranger laughed, while an angry Pip went to watch the men dance.

Buck noticed the outraged look on his son's face. He stopped his class and went to Pip. "What's wrong, Son?"

"Dad, a rude fellow is here and I…"

Buck spied Reggie, the former classmate and military reject who married Laura, Buck's high school sweetheart. Drunk and reeling, a nasty smirk graced Reggie's unshaven face.

"So the hero returns. You have a lot of nerve comin back here. Bet ya thought ya could get Laura, now that we've split. Damn woman, she never stopped talking about you," Reggie growled, staggering closer.

"Reggie, I'm not here to get Laura back. I came because there's an illness in my family. Now why don't you leave? You've had too much to drink."

"Nah. Think I'll insult your limey son again."

"What did you say to my son?"

"Oh, I just called him a little Jew bastard. What cha gonna do about it, *dancing boy?*"

Buck delivered a punch to his midsection, knocking the wind out of him.

"I hate you, all of you!" Reggie shrieked, as he struggled to his feet and wobbled out.

Unaware that he had a captive audience, the men applauded.

"Geeze, Buck, so many of us have been itchin to do that for years," Bobby commended.

He took a deep breath, gathered his thoughts and told the dance class, "If you'd like to continue the classes, we can combine them with the next support group meeting, in a couple of days."

Phil inquired, "Can we invite our wives?"

"I think it's an agreeable request, but just for every other class," Buck responded.

As Buck and Pip left the building, Pip offered, "I've never been called a Jew before and in a negative way. If the Jew hater had been in London, I would have done the same as you. I studied boxing and martial arts at Oxford. Thank you, Dad."

"You're welcome. Sorry you had to experience the likes of Reggie. The bastard's been a plague on this town, long as I can remember. Guess we're a lot alike."

CHAPTER 17: 1964 DANCE THERAPY

After six weeks Buck and Pip fell into a routine. They enjoyed helping the family, hanging with Gram and Grampa but also looked forward to free time.

The Tumas Café became a popular meeting place for Pip and Buck, since Buck's high school and vet buddies stopped there after work.

Gradually, the men appeared less tired and less grumpy. Instead, they seemed to possess more energy and appeared happier.

"My back does not ache so much," Phil praised. "The wife wants to know what happened, says I wake up more rested."

Buck smiled, knowing this would occur. The bunch of overweight men began to tone up muscles and increase lung capacity. They looked forward to more dance activity.

"The old lady wants to come to our next dance session," Bobby commented.

"Mine too. I don't think we can keep them away. I have to admit, it's kinda nice to do something together for a change. We worked hard, raised our kids. This gives us something new to look forward to," Phil reflected.

"I'm flattered, meeting your wife during a couples class would work fine. I'll tell Dr. Bartulas, maybe he'll bring his wife too."

Pip smiled. Seeing his father encourage the men to accomplish something outside of their comfort zones was a miracle in the making. He wondered if similar therapies might work for people with worse breathing issues like Mike, the elderly chap he met a few weeks ago.

Perhaps I need to join my good friend John in the field of medicine? What could I offer Mike and other poor blokes?

The following week, half of the men brought their wives. Buck took advantage of this and encouraged more wives to future sessions. The feminine presence enlightened the atmosphere. The men came freshly shaven, Old Spice and Bay Rum scented the air. The wives found an excuse to have their hair done and get out of housewife attire. Most importantly, everyone was having a good time.

Buck observed the wives and chose the one he felt might be the best dancer. He began with a simple two-step and gradually a few swing steps, which he demonstrated for the rest of them.

Now it was the couples turn to follow. The high school hot shot dance couples were first to follow, then their close friends and finally, with a bit of coaxing, the rest followed. Buck would interject his way into each of the couples and work with the wife, show her a few steps. Occasionally, he would also take the husband and do the same.

One of the couples brought their teen age daughter as a partner for Pip, who enjoyed the chance to join the others, as they all danced.

As time went on, Buck and Pip had to consider ending their visit. Buck and Dr. Bartulas set up a schedule for group therapy and dance therapy on separate evenings.

As Pip helped his dad clean up, thoughts strayed back to John and the chance meeting with Mike.

Seeing what his father had done, he knew it was time to make a decision. He wanted to do something good in this world, and he knew exactly what that required.

CHAPTER 18: 1964 ACROSS THE POND AGAIN

"What do you think, Pip, ready to go back soon?"

"I'm sad to leave my gram and grampa, but ready to get on with my life. Here, read John's last letter. He's doing well in his first year of medical school, it's challenging of course, but he likes it. I'm thinking along those lines myself. I want to make a difference, just as you did."

"Good. I'm proud of you, Son."

"Thanks, Dad. I suppose I wanted to do this all along, but the men from your high school, the vets, even Mike, the chap I met at the train station, all helped in my decision. I think there's a purpose in this life for me. I want to find a way to help chaps like them."

Buck offered, "As soon as we return, let's not waste any time for you to apply. There's room in my flat until you're accepted and have a room of your own."

"I will look for some work until the session begins."

"I could use another set of hands in the studio," Buck suggested.

"Grateful for your offers, Dad. I am getting excited now. When can we leave?"

"Two-three days. I want to make sure Mom and Dad are settled and the dancing sessions continue. Is that okay with you?"

"Of course, Dad. They're in my heart so I'll take a part of them back with me." Pip smiled. He was eager to join his friend John and make his dad proud.

CHAPTER 19: 1965 MEDICAL SCHOOL

After returning to London, Pip applied and waited anxiously to hear the results from his application to Oxford University Medical School.

If all works out, and they accept him, once more, he will be near his best friend, John, but a year behind him.

Pip and John remained close since their days at The Wadsworth School. During the time Pip spent at his grandparent's home in the States, he and John had exchanged letters, and at Buck's expense, allowed his son the privilege of a few long distance telephone calls.

During one of those calls, Pip and John had talked earnestly about a medical career.

"Can you hear me?" Pip inquired.

"A little static on this end, but okay," John responded.

"So...how is your first year of med school so far?" Pip questioned.

"I am up to my knickers in patients, charting and researching the bloody drugs to prescribe."

"Any time for an occasional pint at the pub?"

"Hardly, but I have nurtured a fondness for short naps."

"Good news. My Dad and I will start to leave the 'States' in about 3 days."

"Smashing. I look forward to seeing you soon."

"John...John. I've seen a lot of yanks here with various stages of lung disease. I want to make a difference so I've decided to enter medical school when I get back."

CHAPTER 20: 1966 ROOMMATES

John's roommate, faced with pressures and uncertainty of completing the next few years of medical school, decided to leave. His decision left John by himself. The medical school usually paired students in the same year of study, however, John, an exemplary medical student, convinced his professors to let Pip move in.

For Pip, it was like old times. He and John had been close like brothers the past 10 years. Their history, unlike most young men, had followed a path of sorrow, struggle and abuse.

The two young men often discussed their medical intentions for their future. John talked about cardiology. He saw opportunity for research and prevention of heart disease. Pip's contact in the States with the miners and their lung issues, tended towards respiratory medicine and infectious diseases.

They had already completed three years of pre-clinical coursework in the classroom and laboratory at university. Their medical school required three more years, where they would spend most time in the clinical areas. These next three years will include "hands on" experience with live patients on the various units of the Medical Center. Five more years would follow in a residency program of their chosen specialties.

"Pip, I delivered my first baby this morning. Literally a bloody mess. You should have been there. That poor woman suffered a painfully long labor. She cursed the poor theatre nurse, cursed me and then threatened to castrate her husband."

"I'd hate to be her husband."

"She screamed with each contraction."

"Couldn't they give her something for the pain?"Pip asked.

"They gave her whiffs of gas, it never fazed her."

"Mark my words, she'll most likely be back next year," Pip challenged.

"Ghastly, I say. I'll be happy when this obstetrics rotation ends. Next year, you'll have your turn, just wait. I'm up for a pint. You?" John asked.

"Maybe later. I read in one of the medical journals, that they're funding some research into respiratory diseases. I would jump at the chance to get into that program."

"Overcrowding your busy schedule, old chap, don't you agree?"

"It's a bit over the top, but damn, it sounds intriguing. I'm going to contact the organization so they keep me in mind for future programs."

"Jolly good choice. Do that after the pub. Right now, I need a drink or two," John insisted.

CHAPTER 21: 1966 FIRST OFF SITE CLINIC EXPERIENCE

The medical students shadow attending physicians while treating clinic patients. They participate in taking histories and physicals, interact and observe.

"Sir, I want to listen to your chest." Pip told the patient.

"Say what?"

"Your chest, Mr. Hartley, I want to hear how it sounds," Pip said, moving closer. He listened to the patient's chest while the patient sat quietly between deep productive coughs.

"Eh?"

"The old cock can't hear, he's almost deaf. You must speak up," directed Dr. Westly, as he stood by observing.

"Thank you Doctor. I will."

"First time in the clinics, Mr. Remke? You'll get used to it."

"It is, Sir."

"The dregs of the earth, some of em. They can't breathe, cough up blood and whatever else hides in those black lungs, yet the bastards still smoke."

"So many of them in this condition. Some are young, not much older than me," Pip said, checking the patient's chest.

"The mines, they work in the bloody mines. Put to work as children, some of them. Their parents should be hanged, bastards," Westly stated.

"The best parts of their lives stolen from them. They look old. Physically, their bodies are old. Even their eyes are downcast and weary."

"Mr. Remke, you've described it perfectly. Unfortunately, there's not a bloody damn thing we can do about it. The mines need workers, people need coal for heating and cooking and miners don't have many other choices."

"Sir, why are there so many of them? I estimate that 75% of our pulmonary clinic population are miners."

"Mr. Remke, mining provides the only work in this area. They work, have a pint, come home, clean up a bit, eat, and bonk their wives. Not unusual for them to produce offspring every two years. The cycle of offspring working in mines repeats itself over and over again," Westly informed Pip.

"Hey Doc, I'm coughing up blood. Now do ya believe me?"The man said, his hands bloody as he approached the doctor.

"I believe you, Hartley. I'm sending you home with some medicine. Take it with meals and stop smoking. Tell your boss you need a couple days off to breathe some fresh air. I am writing a note for him."

Reading Mr. Hartley's chart, Pip asked, "How many years in the mines?"

"Twenty five. My dad brought me here when I was ten. Found me a job."

"At ten years old?" Pip asked.

"Yes sir. Me and my dad worked the south shafts, together. Folks needed the money, we had lotsa children." Hartley said, coughing.

Handing the miner a bottle of thick, green liquid, the somber elder physician said, "Hartley, this will reduce your coughing, now don't forget to take it."

Mr. Hartley got up slowly and struggled to catch his breath. Then he gradually removed himself from the clinic examining table.

While Mr. Hartley shuffled his way out, another patient came in. As the sickly figure started to sit on the table, Pip noticed others, lined up to follow.

During Pip's examination of the patient, he thought of his boyhood friend, Rod. His father, a miner, forced him to also work the mines.

Hope he survived. Never did hear from him, thought Pip, as he listened to the congestion clogging the patient's lungs.

CHAPTER 22: 1950 LUCINDA

"Now, now, Lucinda, we always holiday in Newport during the summer. Why change our family routine?"

"Auntie Violet, I can't face another summer without excitement, or activity except the same old boring parties, dull people and annoying small talk. I want to travel abroad. Please! Just this once, Auntie, please!"

"I may love you like my own daughter, but as your guardian, my decision stands, for your own benefit," Aunt Violet declared.

Lucinda placed her arm around Auntie, and while planting a soft kiss on her cheek, whispered in her ear, "Imagine, booking passage on an ocean liner to Europe. Several of my friends from school are sailing with their parents. London, Paris, and Rome, these faraway places, they call to me."

"What about our home in Newport? The servants always prepare for our arrival after your school ends. Prudence dictates we leave the city, soon as possible. Manhattan gets dreadfully hot in the summer. None of our friends stay. They leave for their summer homes," Aunt Violet announced.

"Or travel," Lucinda interrupted. "The *New York Times* advertises transatlantic passages to Europe. The *Queen Elizabeth* offers comfortable cabins and activities during the voyage, just this one time, please. If you don't like it, I promise NEVER to ask again."

"Well...it might be a pleasant change. I agree, our friends, have become frightfully boring. Especially the nouveau riche, like Mrs. Dawkins, if I hear about her husband's promotion one more time, or Mrs. Bight's brilliant grandchild, I will scream."

"See Auntie, I told you so. We both need a change. School is over soon. Do what you can to board passage. Remind the booking agent that my father held seats on the Stock Exchange as well as major transportation companies. This is going to be so exciting!" Lucinda exclaimed, giving Aunt Violet a big hug.

CHAPTER 23: 1950 THE *QUEEN ELIZABETH*

The *Queen Elizabeth* the largest passenger liner ever built at that time, first entered service in February 1940 as a troopship in the Second World War. It was not until October 1946 that she served in her intended role as an ocean liner.

Lucinda's and Violet's accommodations rated beyond first class, perhaps on a par with those of the Duke and Duchess of Windsor, who were frequent guests on the vessel.

Violet oversees the attendant as she unpacks and hangs up their clothes.

"Gently, my dear. Those are very expensive," Violet advises, as the helper removes her expensive formal wear and gently shakes out the wrinkles.

Aunt Violet teased, "So far, I haven't heard any complaints about formal dress for dinner and entertainment."

"Complaints!" Lucinda exclaimed. "Just try and stop me. I love dressing up in my new frocks. Sophie, the buyer from Bonwit's ordered these lovely gowns from the boutique section for me. She knows my size and taste. I don't even have to try them on.

"Oh my...on second thought, do you think I overspent?"

"Probably, but this is a time to splurge, at least a little."

Aunt Violet proceeded to the balcony of their cabin, positioned herself on one of the lounge chairs and stared at the water rushing by the great ship. Her thoughts go back to the time she graduated from Barnard. "Damn. How did my life get so twisted around? I looked forward to teaching." Violet reflected aloud.

From their cabin comes Lucinda's exuberant chattering.

"Auntie. Auntie?" Breaking her thought processes, "Should I wear the blue one or the green one this evening?"

"What? The green one looks fine."

***

Flickering thoughts continue to distract her -- *Sister Martha and her husband died, a vow to care for their child, potential career, husband, children, lost.*

***

"Hair up or hair down? You're not paying attention."

"Sorry dear, wear it up this time," Violet suggested, looking at her.

***

She had a boyfriend, at Columbia. They graduated the same time, planned to marry, she intended to teach while he entered law school. It seemed a good start to their lives as one, until fate stepped in.

"Violet, I'm twenty two. I have four years of law school, a year of clerkship and studying for the bar. I can't do this and be a father figure to your niece as well," her boyfriend lamented.

***

"Auntie, can I stroll the deck and check out our surroundings? You can rest while I'm exploring."

"Yes, I've been stressed with all the preparation for this trip. After you come back, we'll dress for dinner."

***

Now alone, she also remembers Lucinda's inheritance, stipulation as her ward, and control of her estate including the entire twenty third floor apartment on Central Park West. The stately building was located near the Museum of Natural History and convenient to the Alden Hotel where they took most of their evening meals.

"Miss you Martha. Wish you were on this trip with me. I can't believe it's been so many years since the horrible accident took your life. Left me empty, "Violet lamented, gazing at the passing water.

"But I'd trade all of it, just to have you back, Martha."

CHAPTER 24: 1950 CHANCE MEETING

Lucinda strolled around the enormous ship, impressed by the surroundings and glad she had persisted. "No doubt, a good decision. So delighted to avoid spending all summer in boring Newport.

"I need a break before I enter Barnard. Auntie chose the school because she and my mother graduated from there. She always lectured about what a fine school it was for well bred young women," Lucinda told herself.

A cool breeze blew across the ship's deck, as passengers walked the promenade.

"Oops, excuse me!" exclaimed Lucinda, after colliding with another passenger.

"Sorry, my fault, not paying attention. I lost my way, looking about, for the afternoon tea room."

After several awkward seconds, the handsome young man smiled. Blushing, she replied, "I forgive you."

An English accent, she thought, *nice looking, well dressed.*

"Uh...Perkins is the name. Lord Gerald Perkins III, to be formal. Please call me Gerald."

"I've never met a Lord before. Am I supposed to bow or something?" Lucinda smiled.

"Ha, ha. Silly girl. Of course not. Americans become confused with titles, don't let it bother you."

"I am Lucinda. I live in New York City, the US, that is."

"I know, New York City. Just came from there myself. Excuse me, just curious, traveling with your parents?"

"No, my Aunt Violet, I've been her ward after I lost my parents."

"Oh, so sorry for your loss. May I ask, where will you be dining?"

"My aunt said the first class section."

"I'm sure your aunt is taking splendid care of you. Perhaps I will see you in the dining room."

Gerald didn't ignore his racing heart. He found a ship's phone and cancelled his previous engagement with a dowdy Austrian countess, "Hello, Gerald here. Bad news my dear, change of plans beyond my control. I won't be able to enjoy dinner with you this evening. What, room service with your mother. Excellent choice. Again, so sorry, Cheerio."

This Lucinda, hmmm, pretty little thing, rather high spirited, first class, sailing with her ward. Sounds like money. This bears exploring, Gerald thought, as he moved about the ship.

***

Rumor had it; the first class dining room impressed even the most jaded wealth. The huge room housed numerous tables covered in snow white cloth, soft linen napkins, gleaming glassware and sparkling silver. The sounds of soft string and piano music filled the air and calmed the soul.

"A glass of wine, please Auntie. I turned eighteen, months ago."

"Oh all right, just one," Violet conceded.

"How divine. I want to stay on board forever," Lucinda said, looking about the beautifully decorated room.

"Dear child, I agree, but in a few days we disembark to London as our first stop."

"I know Auntie, just let me dream and make it last."

As the evening progressed, they dined on Beluga caviar, Maine lobster and Baklava for desert.

Later, relaxing after their enjoyable meal, Lucinda scanned the room. To her surprise, she noticed a familiar face. "Hmm, the young man I met this afternoon, Lord Gerald Perkins, seems to be chatting with quite a few people, he's like a politician. I thought royals remained aloof," she said to herself.

Whether planned or not, he soon ended up in front of their table.

"Oh, hello again. Lucinda, this must be your lovely Aunt Violet, the one who graciously booked this wonderful passage," Lord Perkins smiled.

In a non approving tone, Violet said, "Lucinda, this young man seems to know you. He also appears to be familiar with my name."

"Auntie, meet Gerald, err...Lord Gerald Perkins. I met him this morning during my stroll. May he join us?"

"Lucinda, you...of course," Auntie rasped.

"My pleasure," Gerald responded with a bow.

"A Lord? What brings you on this passage?" she asked, studying him.

"A holiday as well as a few business matters which needed my attention. Family business matters."

Auntie noticed him fidgeting with a signet ring on his small finger. She wondered why he seemed nervous, maybe hiding something. Filled with caution, she pried, "What kind of work would a Lord such as yourself do?"

"As the last Perkins, I manage my family's estate. Grandfather killed in the war, mother died of cancer, father - his heart, stress of running the Perkins' interests. Went to Oxford. Jolly place. Studied languages, some accounting. Finance comes in handy to manage the estate. Actually, it's rather large."

"How interesting. I'm sure that my Lucinda told you she will attend Barnard College at Columbia, in New York. She will begin her studies in September."

Lucinda, sensing the conversation grew into a contest, chimed in, "Gerald, this is my favorite song…please dance with me? Excuse us Auntie."

Amazed by the cheeky young American, he gave a slight bow of his head towards the aunt and accepted.

They walked to the dance floor and soon glided across black marble to Glen Miller's big band sound of *"I'll Be Seeing You"*.

"Gerald, we don't even know each other and you have been, well…quite forward. Auntie shields me from everything, including you, but the animosity started to give me a headache."

"She appears to be a strong and protective woman."

"She has to be. Aunt Violet safeguards the assets, I inherited from my parents."

"Yes, understandable," agreed Gerald, appearing concerned.

"What about you Gerald? You inherited an estate and title, what kinds of successes and failures do you face in life?"

"First, please forgive my brash manners, Lucinda, but I find you quite irresistible."

"Thanks, but you haven't answered my question."

"Yes, about the successes and failures. I own numerous properties and land in England and employ real-estate professionals, skilled tradesmen and un-skilled service workers.

"However, if you have any understanding of business, you can comprehend the concept of asset rich and income poor. My earnings are derived only from rents and stock market gains.

"With all honesty, depending on the month's performance, I can be, well...poor."

"So, besides our chemistry, what interest do you have in me? Money?" Lucinda grated.

"No, no," Gerald responded. "Only, if we are compatible and fall in love with each other."

"You want to find a rich woman to marry?"

"Yes, but not *just* a rich woman, but a *principled* woman of means."

"Interesting theory, attempting to blend human emotion with a person's economic needs. Look, we'll be disembarking in England soon and you'll be home, back to your old life. Auntie and I will be on vacation in London," Lucinda mentioned, as they danced.

"Lucinda, think about our conversation. It may be a new life for both of us. Will I see you again?" Gerald cooed.

Lucinda planted a light kiss on his cheek, "We'll have to see, won't we?"

CHAPTER 25: 1970 VALERIE PERKINS

"Oh dear, I fear that I won't pass this dreadful exam, I hate chemistry," Valerie said as she shoved her book aside.

"Valerie, cheer up, you know you can do it. Don't you want to graduate from university like your father? Think how disappointing it would be for you and for us. My dear, the Perkins family has a reputation to uphold."

"Mummy, I know, but sometimes I want to run away, be free, help the poor, get my hands dirty," Valerie said, gazing out the huge bay window.

"Nonsense, Darling, how else will you meet a young man you want to marry? The young men today are interested in an educated woman as well as her charm and *position*," her mother answered, sipping her tea.

"But Mummy, you never attended university. You married Daddy when you were eighteen. You told me you and he met on an ocean liner when you traveled with your Aunt Violet."

"That was different. Times are different."

"How so, Mummy?"

"Darling, as I've told you many times, a university education was less common then. Now it's extremely important."

"What does *position* have to do with marriage?"

"Young men today are looking for a woman from a fine family and would fit into their finer circles. That's *position*."

"Mother, sometimes I think you are a snob."

"Darling, I might be, but we cannot marry beneath our station. This is why we send you to Somerville, an exceptional college for young women of finest families."

"Mummy, it's the 70's; women are more independent. They travel without chaperones, they run their own businesses, soon they'll earn as much as men."

"Silly girl, why should you care about these things? Your responsibility is to pass your coursework at university and graduate. Then you'll meet a fine young man and marry. I want grandchildren darling. I'm not getting any younger."

"I want to work, now, have my own flat, get out in the world. I'll...I'll learn to cook," Valerie explained.

"Cook? Even a simple slice of toast is a challenge to you. Valerie, darling, be realistic," Lucinda chuckled, as she nibbled at her biscuit.

"Mummy, I can't talk any longer, must get to class. Love you. Cheers."

She'll never understand me. All she wants is for me to carry on, to live her boring life. Fine young man, good education, prominent family, marriage, children.

With coat and books in arm, Valerie left the estate, taking the chauffeured car to school. While riding in the back of the car, she attempted to study for the chemistry exam, but found herself distracted.

"I want to work, earn my own money, make my own friends. I wish to live my life. Marry the man, I want. Oh, sometimes she just makes me want to scream," Valerie admitted, as she looked at the formulas in the chemistry textbook, frustrated.

CHAPTER 26: 1970 PIP NOTICES VALERIE

Pip's first memorable encounter with Valerie Perkins began at Turf Tavern, the favorite of Oxford students. As usual, he and John arrived in the evening to enjoy a pint to wash down a hearty meal of roast beef, mushy peas and potatoes.

During a lull in their conversation, John noticed an attractive woman at a nearby table fixing her eyes on Pip.

"Pip, don't stare, but you have an admirer -- drop your spoon on the floor and take a peek."

Once Pip saw her, he found it impossible to look away. His cheeks flushed when he noticed Valerie staring back at him.

What kind of woman dares to confront me with her gaze? Maybe a university student, but younger than I am? Her eyes also seemed to hold a message, almost putting me under her spell. He surrendered with a smile.

Soon after, Valerie and her friends gathered their things and proceeded to the front door. When the vivacious, raven-haired woman walked past Pip's table, she returned the smile, darted a last glance and left.

As she left the tavern, Pip, smitten, followed her out the door. He managed to stop Valerie, but fumbled in his effort to talk with her. She, recognizing his clumsiness, asked Pip, if he would like to meet her at a concert in Hyde Park tomorrow. He readily accepted.

Pip arrived on time and scanned the seats until he spotted her in the fifth row, mid section. To his delight, there was an empty seat next to Valerie. Walking down the aisle, he waved to get her attention and asked, "Are you holding that seat?"

She patted the open space and responded, "I'm holding the seat for you, just in case you decided to come."

As he sat down, she confided, "I'm not a big fan of concerts, but attend them to get away from everything else in my life."

During a brief intermission, he mentioned the confrontation at the pub.

Valerie responded with an ambitious nod of her head, tossing fiery raven locks about.

"I must apologize for staring while you ate dinner last night. My parents taught me better. My name is Valerie, Valerie Perkins."

"You didn't offend me. In fact, I appreciated your attention. My mother named me István, uh Stephen after my uncle, my last name is Remke. They nicknamed me Pip. Feel free to call me Pip.

"Pleased to meet you, Pip, she smiled, extending her hand."

After the concert, they spent a long time exchanging stories and joking about funny events in their life. It was as if they'd known each other for years. Pip told her about classes and plans at Oxford. Valerie shared stories about university and over doting parents. Pip also opened up about the orphanage. Valerie offered a hug when he shared the sad parts.

"Valerie, I have never felt so at ease with anyone before, except for John, my best friend," Pip told her.

"I feel the same, but sad about your orphanage and foster care years. You've been through a lot...but your future looks so promising." Kissing him lightly on his cheek, Valerie gave Pip her telephone number and walked to an awaiting cab.

CHAPTER 27: 1970 VALERIE AND MUM

Feeling excited, body tingling, an elated Valerie rushes to the telephone and answers the monotonous ringing. "Mum, so glad you called, I have so much to tell you."

"All ears darling, tell me your great news? Aced the test you fretted about, perhaps?"

"No Mummy, nothing like that."

"What then? Tell me."

"I met the man."

"The man? What man?"

"The man who will be the father of my children."

"What?"

Smiling and continuing in a dream-like voice, "Mummy, I've fallen in love with this chap and wanted you to be the first to know."

"What do you know about him? His family, his aspirations."

"I will find out. When I do, I will let you know."

"Valerie, darling, this sounds absurd. You can't love someone you know nothing about!"

"I do Mummy. I saw him first at Turf Tavern. His eyes met mine and when he spoke, I surrendered. This is the man."

"You mean you haven't formally met? You just saw him and now you plan to bring him into our lives?"

"Not exactly. We spoke briefly at Turf Tavern, and the following day, met at a concert in Hyde Park. I am sure he's the one."

"Heavens."

"Mum, please don't get your knickers in a twist. I will be sensible, but this is the man I want, poor chap, he has no idea."

"Valerie, you've given me a headache. I can't continue this conversation until you come to your senses. I'll speak to your father. Maybe he can reason with you."

"No matter what either of you say, you'll see that I'm right. You will feel the same way, when you meet him," Valerie told her mother before their conversation came to an end.

"I'm late. Bye Mummy. Love you."

CHAPTER 28: 1970 RELATIONSHIP

On a typical rainy afternoon, as he waited for Valerie to meet him at Turf Tavern, Pip wondered, *what the hell have I gotten into? Poor residents like me, chasing a career of internal medicine and hopefully a respiratory specialty, don't have time to think of a woman. No, not just a woman, Valerie Perkins. I neither can spare the time or money to properly woo her. I have no damn business even thinking about it.*

Shaking off her umbrella and hanging up her raincoat, Valerie apologized, "Sorry I'm late, waiting long?"

"N..., no. Just arrived myself," Pip lied.

"Dreadful exam, kept me later than I planned."

Pip inquired, "What kind of exam?"

"Chemistry. Hate the bloody subject, don't know why they require it."

"What do you major in?"

"Education. My major requires chemistry but the symbols and formulas don't make sense," Valerie admitted.

Pip laughed," Having trouble memorizing important terms, understanding logic to the formulas? Been there myself. Maybe I can help."

"Very generous, but I will try your patience."

"Speaking of try, what say we give it a go, my pleasure."

***

One week later

***

"You make it so easy," Valerie said, leaning close to Pip.

"Patience and repetition. It grows clearer when you try and reason it out. A close friend taught me that," Pip answered, noting how intoxicating she smelled.

"I will just have to kiss you, I'm so happy, never thought I might ace this bloody subject," Valerie smiled.

"I won't mind," a blushing Pip replied.

The grateful kiss stirred emotions in him. Pulling her soft form closer, his body reacted, causing him embarrassment. "So sorry. Excuse me. I must go."

"Did I do anything wrong?"

"No, no. Running late, must go. Cheerio," he apologized, holding his coat in front of him.

Once home, Pip found himself immersed in a hot bath. *Romance scares me. Not sure how to handle it. Maybe a talk with John will help.*

After getting dressed, Pip found John studying and asked if they could talk.

"Pip, old chap, what occurred happens every day, quite normal. So...your first time? I mean, shooting your load and all?"

"Bloody yes," Pip said, feeling awkward.

"Look, we both suffered the same humiliations when we lived in Mrs. Savage's foster home. Those bastards had their way with us, never thought about functioning like normal chaps either."

"How did you manage?"

"My friend, Dr. Thomas Youngman, worked with me, a few sessions. It helped."

"You confessed that bodily ravage?"

"You have to get rid of the blooming guilt, not our fault. We had enough problems, as mere orphan boys, until those older bastards sodomized us," John said, looking at his friend.

"I'll think about it. Funny, we never spoke of this before."

"My friend, a whole world of wonderful women waits for our lusty bodies. You need to go back to your girl and have another go at it. I'm sure she understands. They have an effect on us," John winked.

"That she does. She…every time I'm around her, I feel different. And when she kissed me…"

"Don't analyze it, old chap. Accept it and surrender to all its guilty pleasure. Trust me, you'll be better off."

"Yes, that's what I must do, just surrender."

"It's like dancing, except let her lead. She'll know what to do," John assured him.

CHAPTER 29: 1970 JOHN

John's optimistic spirit put a spring in his step in anticipation of the good news he planned to share with his best friend.

He had met with a group of successful physicians from prestigious Harley Street. They campaigned for a young physician to enhance their group with fresh ideas and wealthy patients. They were impressed with his credentials.

Back in his flat, reserved for hospital senior residents, he studied the reflection of himself in a bedroom mirror, "I am quite a descent looking chap and I've come a long way, we both did. Pip's demons, like mine, will haunt him forever unless he accepts help," John said to his reflection, as he thought about the advice he gave to Pip.

Gazing into the mirror, he also recalled his own struggle during the year he met Pip. At eleven years old, fate made them wards of England. Pip came from Stepwell Orphanage and both were placed in foster care on Mrs. Savage's large farm.

Her husband, killed in London's Blitz, left the widow, Mrs. Savage, dependent on foster care boys to help run her farm.

"The foster home sends replacements every year or two," Mrs. Savage said. "Otherwise, they grow too aggressive, when their hormones kick in."

As the new boys, Mrs. Savage placed John and Pip in the care of the older ones. The hooligans not only made them do most of the work, but took other advantages as well. When Mrs. Savage left to pick up supplies, they took turns, sodomizing the younger boys. This went on for at least a year until she discovered what was happening and the authorities intervened.

Those bastards, what they did to us bordered on the worst of crimes, we had no one to stand up for us, just helpless children.

Up until Pip told him about the scene with Valerie, they never spoke about the multiple times they had been humiliated. They had repressed the events and in Pip's case, an otherwise normal encounter, resulted in having to deal with painful memories.

John kept his feelings in tow until he had met Elizabeth, an attractive female resident. Elizabeth had beauty, smarts and possessed an engaging personality. After a few weeks, they finally slept together. More experienced than John, Elizabeth understood his clumsiness. As much as he enjoyed the closeness, he had suffered flashbacks from feelings of intimacy.

He recalled a posting indicating one of the psychiatrists scheduled a paper on sexual intimacy. A hot topic, the auditorium had filled quickly. Dr. Thomas Youngman, who recently passed his boards, researched a generous population of men and women between the ages of 22 and 25. He determined that of the test subjects studied, 35% admitted intimacy issues. His straight forward talk had caused many to come forth with candid questions.

John, a reserved chap, asked to meet with Dr. Youngman in private. The doctor's professional feedback encouraged John to unburden himself and talk freely. Thereafter, he had engaged in weekly one–on-one meetings and found forgiveness. In the end, he discovered absolution of guilt from the actions of others.

"Having kept that all locked up inside me all these years really did me no good. Can't change the past, but at least I can now work towards making a better future for myself," John told his reflection, as he straightened his shirt and readied himself for a night out with his good friend.

"I will encourage Pip to meet with Doctor Youngman and find peace going forward."

CHAPTER 30: 1971 INVITE TO TEA

"Emergency? What emergency? Pip, old chap, it's not your nature to fret."

He shoved the hand written document on fine embossed stationary at John, "Damn, look at this bloody invitation," he said in a panic.

"An invitation for tea? Tea at the estate of Lord and Lady Perkins. Valerie's parents, I assume, sounds like a descent offer," John stated, handing the invitation back to his friend"

"This...this makes me uncomfortable. Like they want to look me over, size me up. See if I place high enough for their daughter, for them, and their bloody friends, damn it," Pip exclaimed, pacing about their flat.

"Old man, you must be daft. You earned a place in the professional social class, a physician, not Harley Street yet, but damn near. Smart, fairly descent looking, in a *rugged* sort of way."

"RUGGED SORT OF WAY! You earned a rugged pasting for your remark," Pip declared, punching John in the arm.

"This solves nothing. We can discuss it like intelligent men, bloody Oxford chaps. It's just tea and idle chatter for a few hours," John said moving about the flat as Pip followed.

"I agree, but until this invitation, everything was okay. Now, I'll be under scrutiny. She hardly ever spoke of their social standing. But then if she did, I never gave it a thought."

"Understandable, but stop fretting. You plan to see Valerie and attend the invite, yes?"

"Yes, of course, I've grown fond of her, quite fond, actually."

"Then, you have no choice." Opening Pip's armoire, "Your wardrobe looks bloody awful. Not one descent suit here," John remarked, flipping through Pip's clothes.

"Pretty sparse, I know. The one suit I owned is in pitiful condition, just old and frazzled and I never replaced it. Working in the hospital and clinics has spared me the need for expensive clothes."

"Wonder where we might borrow one. Too bad, I soar over you by a few inches. What about your father?"

"Not the same size. I stand a bit taller and weigh more than Dad. The dance studio keeps him in shape. By golly, I know who, my Uncle István, Mum's brother, do you remember him?"

"Yes. The Juniper sports car designer. However, as I remember, the newspapers called him by the Anglo version of the name, Stephen," John remarked.

"Guess he's become a proper British citizen. You both seemed about the same height, bet you just might fit, if he doesn't mind?"

"I don't think so. He's offered help over the years. Stephen's a fine chap, but feels guilty about Mum's death. He indulges me to make up for her loss," Pip divulged.

"Better give him a call then," John implored, "an invitation awaits you."

***

"Stephen here, Pip, old boy, good to hear from you. Hold on, let me go to another room, I can barely hear you...okay, better. Now, you have a favor to ask? "Anything, ask. A suit? Of course I can. Any special color? Style? What else? You will need descent shoes to go with it. Why not come here and I can fit you. My pleasure, anytime."

"How exciting. Pip has never asked me for anything. However, the damn sod insisted on needing it in a rush. My tailor can outfit me with a proper wardrobe in just a few days. Now, if I can convince him to drive my latest sports car, let these upper class snobs eat their hearts out," Stephen muttered to himself.

***

Wow. I can't believe Uncle Stephen let me use his new, two-seat convertible. Nearly bored me to death though, reading a part of the owner's manual before I left, but then, he wrote it.

The large size of the new V12 engine impressed Pip, when he left his Uncle Stephen's flat. It was a struggle, not to exceed 80 kph. Although the drive grew tedious, he eventually arrived at Lord and Lady Perkins' estate. Passing a gated entrance with a private drive edged by leafy trees, he observed the manicured shrubs and gardens.

"What the devil does she want with me, a poor resident, struggling, with ambitions of caring for the poor," Pip mumbled while driving up to the house.

"HOUSE, more like a palace," Pip remarked. "What have I gotten into? What am I doing here?" he questioned the whole idea and thought about turning back.

A uniformed gentleman stepped to the car and greeted, "Mister István Remke, Sir?"

Pip thought the man's dignified voice might be fit for the baritone role of Verdi's *Rigoletto*.

Pip nodded and after leaving his uncle's car, wandered into the ante room. "Where is she?" he wondered, searching the room, filled with people.

A sigh of relief expelled from Pip's perspiring body when Valerie appeared. Nonchalant, energetic as usual, she rushed up to him and planted a reassuring kiss on his cheek.

Pip, still feeling a little discomfort, calmed himself and let Valerie lead them into the drawing room.

Although numerous people populated the area, he noticed one man, much too dapper for attending a tea, chatting on the phone.

"Of course, sell the bloody stuff. Move 10% of my transportation stocks out of railroads, into airlines."

Looking up, realizing Valerie's young man has arrived, Lord Perkins ends his conversation and rises to greet Pip.

Looking him over, Lord Perkins takes notice: fairly descent looking, strong jaw, smashing suit, tailor made, shoes polished, auto in the car park -- expensive. He wonders if Pip comes from money. In a short time, he will know everything.

CHAPTER 31: 1971 AFTERNOON TEA

Despite the shock of the affluent estate, array of well dressed people and ostentatious display of food, Pip poised himself enough to stand tall and extend a firm hand to Valery's father. "How do you do Sir!"

"My pleasure, Mr. Remke. My daughter's told me how much she enjoys your company. This occasion gives us the opportunity to finally meet you," he said clasping Pip's hand in a firm grip.

"Thank you Sir! Splendid home you have."

Motioning around the enormous room, "My life started here, as well as my father and grandfather before me. May I show you to the food? We can talk more after you've filled your stomach."

"Thank you Sir, my busy schedule didn't allow me to eat this afternoon. I'll try one of the delicious looking sandwiches."

Pip gazed upon the multiple four-tiered Wedgewood platters filled with finger sandwiches of crust less shapes of bread filled with chicken salad, egg salad, tuna and capers, mystery fillings he failed to interpret. Scones of all kinds, along side of a Royal Brierley footed cut glass bowl filled with clotted cream; small cakes topped with strawberries and whipped cream, made him hungrier than he thought.

A feminine voice startled Pip, "Try the salmon with watercress sandwiches, they are divine and Walters, our beverage man is serving tea."

The attractive blonde extended a hand and continued, "Lady Perkins, Valerie's mother. You must be 'Pip', the one she speaks of so fondly."

He shook her hand with a gentle grasp and no more than three shakes. "Pleased to meet you Lady Perkins. Thank you, don't mind if I do. So many choices."

"Take as many as you like, you look hungry. Do you make your own meals or patronize a local pub?"

"I usually don't have much time to make a meal, maybe take something from the hospital cafeteria or a vending machine."

"Vending machine choices don't sound nourishing," she said.

"For the limited amount of free time we have, it serves the purpose."

"Have you seen Valerie yet? I know she was waiting for you."

"Yes ma'am, she sent me over here for some food."

"I'd like to talk with you further, but I must speak to that chap on the other side of the room, before he leaves.

"Cheers."

"Thank you," Pip replied.

Before he even had a chance to help himself to any of the finger sandwiches, Pip heard, "Tea sir?"

Walters, the white-gloved butler handed him a delicate porcelain cup, "Milk sir?"

"Yes please," he replied, grateful the teacup gave him something to do with his hands as well as a saucer to hold a small sandwich or two that he managed to grab.

Pip started to take a bite of a sandwich and sip of the tea. Thinking he was spared from a dreaded interrogation, Lord Perkins approached, "So Pip old chap, if I may call you Pip."

"My friends call me Pip, please feel free to do so, sir."

"Pip, it is then. I noticed you enjoying those tasty finger sandwiches. However, I think you might enjoy Champaign more than tea. Our man, Walters will start serving in a few minutes. May he wait on you?"

"Yes, please. I usually reserve my Champaign drinking for special occasions. I think this might qualify."

"Lady Perkins and I enjoy a bit of the bubbly at tea time. Makes events like this more...relaxed. Let's go into my study, away from this dreadful noise, do you mind?"

"Not at all, sir," Fumbling with too many items, Pip placed the tea cup down but carried his Champaign and modest saucer of sandwiches. He followed Lord Perkins through the endless halls, lined with fancy framed portraits of what appeared to be, important people. At the end, they entered a study.

Pip scrutinized the spacious room, faced with paneled walls, encased leather-bound books, numerous first editions, soft sepia toned leather chairs, impressive paintings and sculpture. He was about to comment on the exquisite things he noticed when the sound of Lord Perkin's voice brought him back to reality, "Valerie tells us that you plan to practice medicine."

"I do and will complete my residency next year," Pip said, sounding confident.

"You must have plans, a specialty? Where do you intend to practice?"

"Sort of, Sir. Nothing definite."

"Have you started making inquiries, looking for opportunities? Sounds like you've waited too long," Lord Perkins said with concern.

"Well...I have a few ideas and plan to reach out after my next rotation. One goal includes spending three months in Wales, tending to the miners, treating their lung diseases."

Unable to hide his distaste, Lord Perkins stated, "Caring for those 'poor devils' in the mines? How will a residency there gain you an appointment with a proper group on Harley Street?" Lord Perkins asked, his eyes locked on Pip, as if daring him to explain the situation.

Flush-faced, Pip replied, "I haven't considered Harley Street, Sir. In regards to making inquiries, I have talked, numerous times, to the National Health Service about working in their clinics and, yes, helping those 'poor devils'."

A long silence prevailed.

"I believe in wanting to do good...to help people who are suffering. I've observed young men who can hardly breathe, their lives are a living hell. There has to be someone who cares, Sir," Pip replied adamantly.

"I see. And do you expect to make a living doing this?"

"I don't see why not, Sir. Others have done it."

"Interesting," Lord Perkins replies, appearing offended.

Uncomfortable and feeling out of place, "I had better go. I appreciate your invitation and please convey my appreciation to Lady Perkins."

"Wait a minute, Pip. No hard feelings, old chap. Valerie and I never discussed your future plans. You understand, our only child is bloody crazy about you and I want the best for her. I hope you will come back soon so we can talk more."

"Of course," Pip replied as he looks around to find Valerie.

"Excuse me Sir, I need a word with Valerie, "Pip tells Lord Perkins, leaving him at the entrance, impatiently waiting to bid Pip good evening.

Spotting Valerie and taking her aside, "Please meet me tomorrow evening about seven at Turf Tavern. We must talk," Pip whispers, then returns to Lord Perkins.

Walking Pip to the door and viewing Steven's 'loaner car', as the valet pulls it up front, Lord Perkins comments, "Such a good looking car you drive."

"Thank you sir," Pip replied, choosing not to comment on the owner.

CHAPTER 32: 1971 ANOTHER CHANCE – LORD PERKINS AND PIP

"Valerie, why did you ask us to invite a commoner, the bloke, who calls himself Pip? He appears to be just another resident physician, who accepts his lot as a poor doctor, treating diseased coal miners," Lord Perkins chides, sinking into his favorite leather chair in the study. Angrily, he picks up and slams his copy of The *Financial Times* on the table knocking over the snifter of expensive cognac, "Damn," he swears.

"Daddy," Valerie replies as she wipes up the spilled cognac and broken glass, "Pip graduated from Oxford, just like you. Did you tell him about your time at university?" she asked, concerned about her father's comment.

"Of course not, but I did my homework on him, scholarship student, poor, lower class. Really, you could do so much better. Careful, don't cut yourself on the glass," Perkins cautions.

"Pip finished top of his class. He's a brilliant man. Because of his time and patience, I passed my exams in chemistry."

"The young man, this, this Pip tutored you?"

Wringing her hands and walking around the study, Valerie turns and replies, "Yes, as a good friend at first, but it grew into more. I've fallen in love with him."

"Bullocks, child. With so many suitors, you fancy this poor, coal-miners' physician sod?"

"Yes. I fancy him. He aspires to help poor unfortunates with incurable diseases."

"How does one explain the posh car he drove? His Saville Row suit, with the finest fabric. I recognized his John Lobb Shoes, the same kind worn by Prince Charles. How bloody confusing," Perkins pours a fresh snifter of cognac, "How can this poor sod afford a luxury car and custom-made clothes?"

"Pip told me he borrowed the car from his uncle, Stephen Kovács. His uncle insisted on the tailor-made clothes."

"The chap who designed Juniper sports cars? Stephen Kovács' nephew is Pip?"

"Yes Daddy. Pip does not own a car, in fact, he does not even own a descent suit, but he wanted to make me happy by coming to our bloody tea."

"What a phony, a charlatan," Lord Perkins said dismissively.

"Please Daddy, meet him again. Give him another chance," Valerie pleaded, standing in front of him, refusing to leave and let him continue reading until he agreed.

CHAPTER 33: 1971 PIP AND JOHN – RE MEETING LORD PERKINS

"Pip, old friend, why the look?" John asked, after Pip joined him at the Snorting Pig Pub, a favorite of the Harley Street crowd.

"Old Perkins just invited me to join him for a pint."

"Sounds good to me. Never refuse a free drink."

"Well...for starters, I'm just not in the same class. Even though I care for Valerie, I told her it will never work, us, I mean."

With a serious look and tone of authority, John advised, "In a few months, after you take your boards, you can practice medicine on your own. I have been talking to my...ah...senior partners and they want to meet you."

"John, you look the part of a Harley Street physician. Handsome, well groomed, expensive looking clothes...you fit in. I do not. You always had a flair for bigger and better things in life."

"Nonsense," John scoffed. You are brilliant, passionate, a caring physician...and you have me. A respected friend who can recommend you. We need new blood. More and more patients with respiratory issues are coming to see the physicians in our practice," John says, scouting the pub to see who was there.

"Everybody seems to smoke now, just look at the movies and magazines – the stars are pictured with cigarettes between their lips…damn cigarettes take their toll on the lungs with emphysema, lung cancer. Even mothers bring their little ones with asthma, because the parents smoke."

"John, I just don't know. I'll be finishing up with my clinic in Wales. I look forward to working with the Welsh coal miners. My old friend, Rod, lives there somewhere -- if he still lives. Remember, I told you about Rod from Stepwell?"

"I seem to recall, the biracial chap with one leg longer than the other. What about him?"

"I haven't heard from him since we parted in '58. His father appeared and took Rod to work in the mines with him, poor bloke. I wanted to help him somehow."

"Pip, as a child, you had no choice, neither did he. Like us all, I'm sure he found a way to survive."

"I hope so. Poor Rod, I sure hope he's alright."

"Pip, you have a more pressing issue right here…your predicament with Lord Perkins. Meet the old cock, listen to what he says. Remember your strengths and how much you've accomplished. You have nothing to be ashamed of. He's not better than you, Pip. Remember that. And if you truly love Valerie, as you say you do, then you'll have to fight for her," John explained as he emptied his pint of ale.

CHAPTER 34: 1971 TURF TAVERN

Dreading the encounter with Lord Perkins, Pip contrived a fitting defense on his way to Turf Tavern. Passing under the Bridge of Sighs with a few twists and turns plus narrow passages, he finally spotted the tavern's familiar green door handle.

It's not too late to turn around, Pip thought, what the hell, I faced worse people at the orphanage and foster home, this will be easy-peasy. He took a deep breath, pulled open the door and proceeded inside. Oblivious to the low ceilings with exposed beams, the rustic wooden tables, the mouth watering smell of fish and chips, he focused on the meeting with Lord Perkins.

Pip entered the pub, only to find Lord Perkins already there.

"Don't worry, you still have a few minutes, I arrived early. You know, I came here as a student, a lifetime ago. The old buildings, trimmed grass and shrubs on campus, bring back pleasant memories."

Pip sat down across from him, trying to remain confident.

Raising his glass, Lord Perkins asked, "I have a head start. You like Watneys'?"

"Sure, one of my favorites. I'll take a pint."

"Good. Also, if you don't mind, I'll order a plowman's lunch for both of us. A tasty meal, as I remember."

"Yes, sir. It's one of the tavern's most popular items."

Perkins motions to the server, "Over here. Two plowman's lunches and two pints of Watneys."

"I thought we might talk better here, away from everyone else. So...tell me about you, family and work. Valerie said, "Your father is *a dancer*."

"Yes, a dancer, but so much more. My father came from a proud family of bricklayers in a small Pennsylvania community, back in the States. His father handed down a legacy to carry on the trade, which is considered part of the craftsmen class," Pip stated, looking around the pub.

"Ahh, food's here. Thank you, looks good," Lord Perkins says to the server. He turns to Pip.

"And the dancing? How did this come about?"

"If you don't mind, I'll come back to it later. For many years, after the war, he...was unaware of my existence."

"You mean to tell me, he didn't know, he sired a son?"

"Well, like many young Americans at that time, they chose to serve their country. My father was one of those men."

"Of course, go on...go on," Lord Perkins impatiently cleared his throat.

"He proudly served as a tail gunner in the 8th US Army Air Force. Received several distinguished service awards for bravery in battle, rescued some of his crew mates and survived the wretched POW camps."

"Tell me more," Lord Perkins encouraged.

"When my dad came to England in the 50's, looking for me and work, the trade unions made it difficult for Americans to find work as a bricklayer.

Fortunately, before my father came to England, he pursued training as a ballroom dancer, as a hobby, for several years, and later excelled as a dance instructor. He worked days as a bricklayer, then performed evenings and weekends as an Arthur Murray dance instructor. He won numerous awards along the way.

He stopped looking for work as a bricklayer in London and with the help of a family member's endowment, opened a dance studio here."

"Dance studio? Courage and brilliance on his part. Was it successful?"

"Yes sir, he took his studios to an international level, expanding to two countries."

"Him, I see. Now, your mother…she was a *nightclub singer*?"

The second round of drinks arrive. Pip takes a few generous sips and begins to loosen up.

"My mother was Ilona László. Yes, she sang at a popular nightclub on the West End."

"She doesn't sound English!"

"No, she was born in Hungary. My mum studied voice at the Frantz List Academy of Music in Budapest, hoping to become an opera singer."

"How did she reach London?"

"For reasons too involved to explain now, the threat of death by Nazis, forced her to leave occupied Hungary. Bravely, my mum escaped to Zurich and stayed with friends of her Uncle Gabe, Gabe Kovács, her father's younger brother," Pip explained, then drank more of his ale.

"Fascinating. Sounds like a brave young woman."

"I would say so. Mr. Brunner, Uncle Gabe's friend and classmate at Oxford.

"Your Uncle Gabe was an Oxford graduate?"

"He was and a champion football player. Later became a managing partner in the law firm his father-in-law established."

Staring in the distance, Lord Perkins talked out loud to himself, "Gabe Kovács," champion football player and famed Oxford supporter? Is it...is it, the same Gabe Kovács that funded a wing of one of our libraries? He and Karl Brunner, former President of the Swiss Central Bank?"

"Yes sir. My mum's Uncle Gabe. Mr. Brunner and he were best friends."

"Karl Brunner? Karl Brunner, he must be the philanthropic chap who funded scholarships to outstanding young men at Oxford?" Perkins mumbled.

Continuing with his story, "When my mum reached Uncle Gabe's home, it created friction with his wife. He unexpectedly died and poor Mum was thrown out onto the streets. She found her way to a nightclub and a job washing dishes."

"Horrors!"

"I am told, while there she learned English and sang while she worked. The manager heard her and offered a job, since their singer was leaving."

"Fancy that, by damn."

"There, she met my dad and later, I was conceived. He was called away for the D-Day mission and she did not have the opportunity to tell him about me. That was the last time they saw each other."

"Dreadful...eat up, Pip. Is the meal okay?" Perkins motions, "Waiter, another pint, please."

Wiping away tears with the back of his hand," Excuse me, I need a moment."

"Take your time," Lord Perkins offered.

"Mum made friends with this elderly couple, Mary and Mike. To make ends meet and allow her to work, we moved in with them and they cared for me."

"I say, clever woman, your mum."

"Except for the day she wanted to buy rabbits from Smithfield Market, it was bombed. That's...(taking a moment to compose himself)...when I lost my mum. The bloody V2's. She...she died along with so many others. The authorities put me into an orphanage after Mary died...Mike died first. Stepwell Orphanage, it was dreadful. After that I was shipped into foster care. There I met my best friend, John."

"John, your physician friend? John, who joined the prestigious Wellesley Medical Group?"

"Correct. On Harley Street, he's trying to tempt me to join them."

"How interesting? How did you and your father finally connect?"

"A letter from my mum, someone sent it to him years after she died. First time he knew he had a son."

"I say, a bit of a shocker there."

"For both of us. It definitely was a challenge. We've become good friends now, in fact we're very close."

"You did not eat very much," Lord Perkins comments.

"Yes sir. I just eat slowly. It's very good."

"You have an uncle, I understand, designs cars for Juniper. I read about his success."

"That was his car I drove to the tea…he insisted."

"Yes, Valerie told me. His clothing too?"

"Uncle Stephen would not take no for an answer. My suit was the work of his tailor. Uncle Stephen and I are close as well."

"Valerie mentioned he fought in the Hungarian army."

"He did."

"Hungary merged with Germany as part of the AXIS. They fought against us during the war, bloody bastards!" Perkins said, banging his fist against the wooden table.

"Whoa, sir!" Pip reacted, "Uncle István, er Stephen had no choice, the alliance occurred after he volunteered. He fought in Stalingrad and was captured by the Russians."

"Terrible plight, poor bloke. I suppose it can't be held against him. Bloody Hitler, Bloody Russians."

"He learned about my mother's death and my existence after he returned to Budapest."

"So much tragedy. I read about his success, it was in the news and some of the trade magazines. A few of my friends own his latest model. They let me drive it a couple of times. Extraordinary car."

Interrupting Lord Perkin's rambling, "Both my father and uncle did well, all on their own. I am proud of them," Pip stated, nearly done with his ale.

"Yes, of course. Do you feel that you could do as well?"

"What do you mean?"

"Support a wife…a child or two. Will you earn enough to support a family?"

"I never thought of it. My concentration has been on completing my residency, passing my boards. I take them in three months," he pauses, holding a forkful of food near his mouth.

"A full-fledged physician in three months," Perkins emphasized. "You mentioned your friend John, with the Wellesley Group on Harley Street. Dr. Stuart Wellesley is a former classmate. We've been friends since university. I could put in a word..."

"Sir, I did not intend to pursue a position on Harley Street."

"Does my daughter Valerie fit into your scheme of things?"

"Of course. I care about her. I care about her a great deal. She's an amazing person. I will do my best to assure she is happy," Pip replies.

Motioning for another drink, Lord Perkins emphasized, "My boy, I strongly suggest, if you consider marrying my daughter, you had better *plan* for a future on Harley Street."

Pip, angry, wanting to tell Lord Perkins that he will not let anyone decide his expectations – instead, chewed his food and thought about Valerie. He knew he had her heart and support, and that was all that mattered.

CHAPTER 35: 1971 ROD, SOUTH WALES

Each deep breath triggered a persistent hack, dislodging thick black mucous. Each episode brought Rod temporary relief, until it started all over again. Black vapors of coal dust, the microscopic remnants which cozy themselves into crevices of his lungs, have sealed his doom, the same fate of his father and coal miners before him. Black lung they called it. The unlucky ones got this disease after working in coal mines for 10 or more years.

Thomas, one of the older miners offers, "Have a bacca, Rod. Chewing it helps to keep dust from getting into your lungs. Here's an extra twist if ya want it."

"No thanks, Thomas. I'll be ok, soon as I get some, get some...air," he coughed again.

"It happens to all of us sooner or later. How long ya been working here in the mines?"

"Since I turned fourteen. My dad found me the job."

Adjusting the lamp on his helmet, he focused on the younger man's face, "He work here too?"

"No longer. Died five years ago."

"How old?"

"Forty five, forty six, there abouts."

"Hmm, still a young man."

"Doc said 'his lungs gave out', besides, he smoked and drank too much. Loathed the mines and hated his bloody life, even more," Rod said, then broke out into a fit of coughing that shook his body.

"Easy to do here, working in the mines. Up and ready by five, hardly time to take a few swigs of tea for breakfast."

"I know, Thomas. I can hardly manage the long walk to the pub to catch the double-decker to work. The blasted routine almost kills me. I slip off the clean clothes and change into pit clothes to be ready by seven. This morning, when I walked over to the lamp room and picked up a battery it seemed to weigh a ton," Rod admitted, his skinny body shaking from the fits of coughing.

"Worked in the mines for twenty five years, son, and I'm still alive. Lucky, I guess. No matter how many years you work here, it doesn't get any easier. Every miner has a choice, the colliery or the poorhouse."

"Company coal owns our life. I don't know how to do anything else," he admits, then coughs again. "I'll probably die young, like my dad," he adds before another coughing fit claims him.

"Son, you ought ta get your chest checked. Clinic will open next week and I'm going. Come with me. I'll tell the boss."

"Thank you," Rod says, between coughs.

CHAPTER 36: 1971 ROD IN HIS FLAT

Returning to his empty flat in the village, Rod stoked the coal stove to heat water for his bath.

Bath. What a laugh, he thought, *tepid water dumped into a washtub, a disappointing luxury of the day for me.*

"It might be nice to have a woman waiting for me with a hot meal and bath. Someone to ask about my day," he says to himself.

His skin pained fiercely after the hard scrubbing of the black layers of coal dust, with some still not removed. It seemed to embed itself into his very flesh, becoming part of him. Sitting back in an overstuffed chair, he thought about his life. His skin still smarting, reminded him of the beatings with Master Stepwell's leather strap.

"Damn, those evil people," Rod mumbled. He thought about his life at Stepwell Orphanage, where Mr. Stepwell and his horrible wife tortured and abused the boys.

During his stay, Rod bonded with Pip, the one and only friend he made in his entire life. However, their friendship ended when his father showed up and abruptly took him away, "I never even had a chance to say good-bye."

He thought of when they fantasized about being claimed. Asked for by their parents. Even one parent. Better yet, adopted by a loving couple. Welcomed into their lives and showered with love. Good night stories, hot porridge and fresh fruit, warm kisses, a mommy and daddy saying 'I love you' and an affectionate puppy to cuddle.

Funny, how it all worked out. He imagined his father as a big strong heroic type, not some cripple with a cane. In all fairness, his dad had suffered an injury during the war.

Born of university-educated parents in Georgetown, British Guiana in 1922, they brought him to London, where his father taught school in London's East End. Rod's father attended university for two years and while there, he met and fell in love with a white woman. They married, and several years later, she gave birth to Rod.

When war broke out, his dad joined the RAF and left before Rod's first birthday. He only knew what information his mother had told him, before she died. Rod never met his father, until one day he showed up at Stepwell and took him to South Wales.

After the war, his father stopped looking for work, because of race and disability. By chance, he met an old RAF buddy at a pub patronized by fellow veterans. From the chap, he learned about mining jobs in South Wales near Cardiff. Until his death, Rod and his father had lived together in the small flat.

At the end of the day, like the days before, Rod performed his nightly ritual. Raising a small glass of cheap whiskey, he toasted his dad. "Miss ya Dad. I know you're in a better place than this hell hole."

CHAPTER 37: 1971 ROD MEETS AN OLD FRIEND

The next day, under duress, Rod prodded himself to dress and catch an early double decker to the clinic. Rod knew if he ignored the symptoms much longer, his lungs, over time, would give out, same as his father's.

Assuming he had arrived early enough to be one of the first in line, he had planned on returning to the mines for a few hours of work. The young miner relied on every pound in his weekly paycheck. "Bloody hell! Looks like a hundred others had the same idea," he mumbled, seeing so many others there as well.

Rod remembered his father's attempt to explain what had taken place in his own lungs. *'When ya breathe in coal dust, pockets of cells, trap the dust. The pockets get bigger and bigger. When ya try to breathe out, your lungs can't expand easily. The enlarged pockets block the flow of air.'*

I didn't pay any attention to his explanation; it makes a hell of a lotta sense now.

Damn, I can't wait much longer. Breathing seems worse and my stomach just started to growl. The other poor blokes ahead of me sound as bad, raspy breathing and coughing their fool heads off.

Shifting his weight, my back hurts like hell, I should forget the whole idea. Wait, they just called my name -- good.

By the time they yelled for Rod, weakness from standing so long and hunger, took over. He struggled to keep his balance. A firm but kind voice called out, "Here, old chap, let me give you a hand."

Surrendering his pride, Rod accepted the strong arms which lowered him into a chair. "You look like you could use some water. Hang on, I'll bring it to you, straight away."

"Thank you, kind sir." He notices the chap's white coat and corrects himself. "I mean, Doctor."

"Appreciate your respect, but I won't earn that title for another couple of months. My name is István Remke. Mr... (looking at the clipboard in his hand)...Mr. Gardner. Gardner, hmm, I knew a chap with that name, many years ago."

Gulping the cold water, Rod smiled as he studied the face of the kind young chap. Suddenly, tears well in his eyes with possible recognition.

"Relax, old chap, I haven't even examined you yet. Your pulse is racing. You appear to be in pain."

Rod, awe struck, stares at the young man before him.

"You're staring, sir. Do you need a moment?"

In an uncertain voice, he replies, "You remind me of a bloke I once knew, a long time ago."

Teasing the humble patient, as he looks over his deformed body, with one leg longer, "An old friend, eh? A descent chap, I hope. How did you know him?"

"We were together in the same orphanage."

Thoughts raced through Pip's head. *Can it be?...No...it's not possible. The local authorities placed me in an orphanage at an early age. My mum died and they thought my dad was...*

"An orphanage?"

"Yes, sir. Stepwell Orphanage."

"They placed *you* in Stepwell Orphanage?"

"Dastardly place. They treated us worse than animals."

The mention of Stepwell made Pip stop. As his heart abruptly raced, haunting memories flooded his mind.

Starvation, beatings, torture. Pip thought he had repressed that wretched part of his life. His survival at Stepwell depended on the camaraderie forged with Rod, his first and only friend in that hell hole. Steadying himself, he checked the patient's given name and date of birth. "Rod…Rod Gardner." *Dear God, this shabby, sickly bloke can't be my old friend Rod? He remembered overhearing a conversation, when Rod's father came for him at Stepwell. 'You're coming home with me so I can take care of you. In two years, when you're fourteen, you can work in the colliery with me.'* Rod's father had told him, and that had been the last time Pip had seen him.

The appearance of an elderly relief physician, who came on duty, brought Pip back to reality. He took Pip aside, interrupting the exam. "Mr. Remke, I'll assume responsibility for the next shift. I'm Doctor Willis. By the way, nice work taking care of our miners. I've heard good things about you."

"Thank you, Sir. I'm glad to be of assistance."

"Well…Remke, over time, you'll find we perform little or no preventative medicine. By the time they reach our clinic, their lungs have scarred and turned black, like the bloody coal they mine. In case you develop an interest in treating patients with pneumoconiosis or black lung disease, the clinic is looking for a young physician who can continue our work with these unfortunate bastards. Let's talk sometime," Dr. Willis said, looking at the chart in his hands.

"Excuse me...uh...Dr. Willis, I'll move this patient into another examining room so I can finish checking out his lungs. If okay, you can bring the next patient in here and start your shift."

"Mr. Gardner, I'll move you down the hall, to the next room, if you don't mind. Follow me please," Pip said, giving Rod an odd look.

Pip took Rod into a more private area and asked him to sit on the examining table. He placed his two hands on the shoulders of the shabby miner and stared into his eyes. "Now, tell me your friend's name, Sir."

Rod responded with a choked up, hoarse reply, "Pip. I can't remember his last name, but I called him Pip," Rod said, looking into the eyes of his old friend.

Standing before his patient, a teary-eyed Pip draped his arms around Rod and lamented, "Rod, it's me, Pip. I can't believe it. My old friend. You're right here in front of me. All these years."

Coughing, firmly hugging his friend, "Oh my god. Pip, I knew it had to be you. I prayed for this moment, to see you once again."

"Oh, I thought about you as well...so many times," Pip countered, holding his friend close.

"For years, I wondered about you, always, in my thoughts. With your help, I survived. A miracle. A true miracle, my friend," Rod said, still holding onto Pip, not wanting to let go.

"We have so many years to catch up on. But first, your medicine. Cough syrup, pills, along with instructions and a return appointment. You need treatment and must keep this appointment. Promise?"

"I will. Promise," Rod agreed, looking him in the eye.

"One more thing."

"Yes?"

"A meal somewhere. Soon. Whenever you can take a day off. I'll make time."

"Yes, yes, this weekend. For a change, I have Saturday free. The company scheduled maintenance so our crew can't work."

"Okay, Rod. I'll ask someone at the clinic to exchange their day off so we can meet. You tell me where and what time."

Pip stops for a moment and hugs his long lost friend goodbye. As Pip steps back, he hides a bad feeling, Rod is frail, very frail, almost like a skeleton, but Pip chooses to focus on the positive news that they will soon spend some time together.

They walk toward the lobby, where Pip sees him off.

"Pip, good to see you again, I thought about this moment for years."

"Same here my friend. I never forgot you," he replied, and they clasp hands before parting.

CHAPTER 38: 1971 THE LAST MEAL

A few days after meeting with his oldest friend, Rod, Pip reaffirmed his desire to treat and care for unfortunate coal miners with lung diseases. Knowing well the ultimatum Lord Perkins gave him, however, his heart told him what he needed to do.

Muttering to himself as he records his findings on patients' charts, "Will Valerie accept my decision? My residency finishes after this clinic. The plan seems simple enough…take the boards and accept an assignment in South Wales. We can work it out… Valerie said how much she loved me."

Saturday afternoon, Pip met Rod at the Bleeding Horse, a local pub where miners go on payday or when they can sneak away from their wives. A downtown location made it convenient and they served good, affordable food. He sensed Rod had not eaten a decent meal in a long time. "Try the roast beef and mash, I guarantee you'll love it."

"Sounds good," Rod said.

"A couple of pints?"

"Of course. Thank you," Rod agreed, coughing.

As Pip and Rod enjoyed the meal, they reminisced about old times, good and bad. Rod also provided insight in vivid detail regarding the life of a coal miner.

Pip initially held back on stories of his good fortune so as not to make Rod feel inferior, however, Rod wanted to hear as many details of Pip's life at Oxford, medical training, everything since he left Stepwell. He hung on to each word, begging for every segment of Pip's life after that sad good bye many years ago.

Pip began with the saga of Mrs. Savage and the abusive life as a foster child in her home. "At least I received help, which placed me into Wadsworth School. I met John there, another foster child and we became friends. John now practices medicine in London."

"Good show, you survived and moved on, eh?"

"Yes, then my father and uncle, found me at Wadsworth."

"Bet it surprised the hell out of you," Rod said, drinking his ale.

"Without a doubt. I didn't know how to handle it. My father in particular."

"What happened to him all those years?"

Pip explained his father's long search for him and how close their relationship has since grown.

"Rod, about your father, I remember when he took you away. I didn't have a chance to say goodbye. I cried for days. I hardly ate or slept and felt all alone."

"Me too. I also recall the evil bastard, Stepwell. He took real pleasure in torturing us. I heard he had a nasty stroke which paralyzed him. Can't even wipe his own ass. Serves him right," Rod stated, his face and eyes looking old.

Pip ordered another round.

The ale relaxed Rod and he opened up about his father, "He remained unemployed for months so he resorted to the mines. The coal company took his life, like it will take all of us. His two year university education didn't help him any, he needed at least two more years to be hired as a teacher. I also heard about the local schools, they didn't want a black man teaching their children," Rod said bitterly. "Forget the fact he served England as a member of the RAF during the war and his country recognized him as a hero. Local businesses rejected him for white collar jobs. When my father started getting sick, from working in the mines, he grew frustrated, then depressed, and in the end, gave up. He accepted the reality, his future offered only work and death in the mines."

"I can only imagine how grim those times turned out, Rod."

"It spiraled down from there, Pip. He drank and smoked more, plus stayed at the pub longer. I'd make dinner and it just would go cold."

Pip continued to let Rod go off on a tangent. As he rambled, Pip made a vow to help…not only Rod, but other miners like him.

"I cared for my mum when he left to fight for our country. I remember being a wee lad when she took sick, I even cooked for her. Bloody cancer took her away from me. Beautiful woman, my mum," he spoke, while crying uninhibited manly tears. "I buried both of em."

"Did you ever have a good relationship with your dad?"

"In the beginning he encouraged my schooling. I reveled in learning, started to make friends and the teacher liked me because I excelled at mathematics. You remember how much I liked mathematics."

"Of course I do, old chap," Pip said smiling.

"The reading slowed me down, but I started to improve. However, when I turned fourteen, he pulled me out of school. 'Time for ya to earn your keep!' he shouted. I didn't think he intended to do it, since my father studied at university for two years. When I mentioned it, he raged, 'School won't get ya nowhere, look at me!'

"I tried to convince him, but he never listened. I said goodbyes to classmates and within a week, the coal company hired me at the colliery. After several years, I started to spiral downward, just like my father," Rod explained, sadness in his voice.

"Bloody awful. He just up and denied you an education?"

"Yeah, as his health turned worse, he started to drink more. He saw me as a liability, not as his son or even someone to keep him company in the evening."

"God awful thing to live through, Rod."

"Uh, huh. Even though I cooked the meals, cleaned the house and washed our coal dust infested clothes, my father just wanted to stay at the pub until the place closed and then he'd stagger home. Eventually, he done himself in."

"Wish I had known, I might have helped."

"Nah, doubt if anyone had the gift to help him. He fell too far."

"You never married?"

"No, it didn't seem right."

"Why not? I've noticed pretty girls in the village."

"Maybe so, Pip, but even if I found the right one, at some point, she might have wanted to meet the old man. Real impressive, huh, with the wrenching and coughing and pissing his pants."

"A terrible situation, but you have time, don't give up." Pip encouraged.

"If my damn lungs hold out. Just breathing wears me out."

"I understand. I want to help you. Let me try."

"How?"

"I'll arrange for oxygen you can use while sleeping. You can come to the clinic for twice daily breathing treatments."

"I can't afford time away from the mines. They won't pay if I don't work."

"I'll look into the company policy. There has to be some compensation for a miner who has a pulmonary illness. Leave it to me, old friend."

Rod's eyes tear. "Thanks, Pip. Just like old times. I don't feel so alone anymore," he said, raising his drink, and both friends toasted a long lost friendship, found.

CHAPTER 39: 1971 TRAGEDY

Pip explored the sick day policy for miners. The organization allowed limited sick time for miners who temporarily could not work. A miner who was totally disabled, would be terminated with a small pension that barely covered their daily living expenses.

In Rod's case, the mine he worked needed experienced young men. Their policy allowed partial coverage for treatment, with the exception they were able to return to their jobs.

Pip arranged for Rod to have several full weeks off with treatment. Aside from the medicine, positive pressure treatments, twice daily at the clinic and an oxygen setup at home when he slept. After that, if symptoms let up, he could continue with treatments three times a week, then two and only periodically if needed. He also was issued a mask with a dust filter.

The mine boss complained to Pip's superior, but Pip defended his treatment. The mine boss finally agreed after Pip convinced him that it would improve Rod's productivity and he would continue to work longer. He also recommended that the mine boss purchase masks with filters for all of the miners.

Rod was grateful for the treatment, more so because his best friend arranged for it. Since Pip often administered some of the treatments, the men shared precious time together. They swore to never to lose touch again and Pip promised himself that when he is a full-fledged physician, he will take Rod away from the blasted mines.

"Think I can increase my work hours yet? My supplies are running low and I have bills to pay," Rod asked, concerned.

"Your progress is improving. The medication and breathing treatments are certainly helping. Next week, you should be able to return," Pip reassured him.

Feeling pleased with the outcome of Rod's treatment, Pip cheerfully opened up the clinic to greet the onslaught of miners. "So many like Rod and they all need treatment. That's why I'm here. It's the right place for me," Pip said, preparing himself for the work he knew was ahead of him.

Suddenly, the mine alert sounded. The men reacted, "What the hell happened? Mine cave in? How many hurt?"

The clinic nurse called out, "Get the trolley, move it, move it!" she hollered to Pip.

Pip grabbed his medical bag and dashed towards the mine. He joined the triage team to identify the injury status while some started to remove the injured miners. "Head wound, needs dressings, looks like his leg is broken; watch his arm, badly damaged, this poor chap...where's that bloody ambulance?" Pip shouted, frustrated.

As he continued making his way into the mine, checking the casualties, he heard groans from one of the miners. "Nurse, this patient, he's still breathing, he's in pain. Help me turn him over so I can examine him."

The injured man, his face, almost unrecognizable by soot, opened his eyes. A moment of consciousness made him realize he was looking at his oldest friend. "Pip, Pip, I feel so cold. Narrow passage in the tunnel, dislodged big pieces of rock. Fell on me. Men trapped," he coughed, "Couldn't get away in time. Hurts like hell."

Recovering from the shock of seeing the extent of Rod's injury, Pip applied pressure to Rod's head and covered the gaping wound with dressings from his bag. "Rod, stay with me, please stay with me. Oxygen here! STAT! We need a stretcher! He lost a lot of blood! Going into shock! We're going to lose him! Where's the bloody ambulance, this man needs surgery straightaway! Damn it!" Pip cursed, as he kept the pressure applied to his friend's wound.

Pip's plea fell on deaf ears. The ambulance arrived, but it was too late. Too late for the frail biracial boy with unmatched legs, who cried himself to sleep at night in the orphanage. His sad life had been filled with too many years of abuse and torment and trying to survive the challenging mines. He had appreciated living long enough that his wish to see his best friend became a reality. Never expecting it to end, dying in his arms.

CHAPTER 40: 1971 DR. WILLIS, AN OFFER

"Mr. Remke, I am so saddened to hear about your friend. The staff told me about your childhood friendship and how you reconnected after so many years," Dr. Willis offered, "I thought we could talk better here in the pub. Whiskey?"

"Yes, thank you. It's uncanny how our lives crossed. His life was so tragic, poor old chap." Pip said before breaking down.

"Here, here, you could not have helped him at the stage his body was in."

"If only I had arrived here sooner. I probably could have. Poor bloke. I...I feel so helpless," Pip admitted nursing his drink.

"Mr. Remke, as tragic as it was to lose a long time friend, I need you to think ahead about your own career. I looked at your paperwork and saw that you will be leaving us in two weeks. What do you think of our operation here?" Dr. Willis asked.

Attempting to focus on the question, "It's well run, under the circumstances," Pip stated, his eyes scanning the faces of some patrons at the Bleeding Horse.

"Fair answer. How would you improve it?"

"Sir, realizing the restrictions, there needs to be better ventilation in the mines. It would be difficult, but I've been reading how other countries accomplished this."

Pip went on about safety for the miners and other quality issues for the mines.

"Go on."

"Dr. Willis, the entire quality of life here needs improvement. I'm looking at future generations and how long the mines will be operational. They should have a library, education, even a family clinic, when family issues occur."

"Mr. Remke, your suggestions are refreshing. Reminds me of myself at your age," Dr. Willis admitted, finished his drink, and ordered another round for both.

"Sir?"

"I had all kinds of thoughts and dreams for the welfare of our miners when I started working here."

"And what happened?"

"The wheels of the Mining Industry turn slowly. So much politics. It will take the vision and perseverance of a young man like you. I've seen it happen. Changing the subject, are you married?"

"No, not yet. I plan to when I return to London."

"Would your wife be happy living here?"

"Have not given it a thought. I'm sure she would be happy wherever I am based."

"Are you married?"

"Twice. Divorced twice. Each time my wife was excited at first. She had all kinds of plans," Dr. Willis said, his voice trailing off.

"What happened?"

"Social life for one. No comparison to London. Not a lot of culture in this area."

"Hmm."

"If you like parties and social events, forget about it. One's life revolves around the miners and the mines. Your wife's life will also.

"I can count the times I had an uninterrupted sleep without someone pounding on my door with a crisis of some sort in the middle of the night. Doesn't make for a good marriage. In my case it didn't make for two marriages."

The waitress arrived with two more whiskeys, placing both on the table before leaving.

"I plan to retire in a year and if you are interested, I would recommend you for the position. First, think about your marriage and if yours could survive," Dr. Willis added.

Pip gave the offer some thought. His relationship with Valerie seemed solid enough. She told him many times that she would follow him and his career 'to the ends of the earth' if necessary. Up to this point there had never been any question. On the other hand, her folks had other ideas. Maybe Lady Perkins would listen to reason, but not Lord Perkins.

Pip finally placed a call to Valerie. It was good to hear her excited voice. "Pip darling, I miss you so much. I can't wait until you come home. I'm so lonesome without you."

Hardly able to interject a word in edgewise, he let her rant about school, and hints about wedding plans after he finishes. He then told her about the offer. A dead silence at the other end of the phone before Valerie spoke, "You mean that after we're married, we would move to South Wales, near the mines?"

"Sort of, there are lovely homes and available land not too from the mines…we could build."

"You would have to travel to the mines every day to take care of coal miners?"

"Coal miners and their families. They are the hub of the community and the reason the job opportunity exists. I see opportunity here to improve work conditions and the health of the miners. Also, the young people, so many are leaving to get away from the mines. If they had a better education system in place and job training, maybe they would stay and help their communities," Pip said excited.

"What would I do while you work in the clinic or busy yourself with other projects?"

"There are families and you might become acquainted with the women whose husbands work, not only in the mines, but some own shops. They have a school; you might want to see if they need a teacher…you always said you might teach someday. I'm sure you would find things to keep you busy while I am at the clinic."

"Darling, this so much to process now. Let me think about it first, "Valerie said.

"Of course. I won't do anything until I hear from you."

When he hung up the phone, he realized there might be a conflict. He never gave it a thought that Valerie would influence his professional life. Within a matter of minutes the telephone rang back.

"Remke here."

"Remke?" A harsh voice called. "Remke, Lord Perkins. On no uncertain terms will my daughter join you in your crusade to save the coal miners, do you understand me?"

"Sir?"

"Remke, if my memory serves me, we had a discussion at the pub a few months ago."

"I realize that. This offer was just made to me and I wanted to discuss it with Valerie first," Pip explained.

"I'll make it simple. If you want to marry my daughter, then you will need to return to London and consider the Harley Street offer. Do I make myself clear? Goodbye Remke."

The phone was slammed so hard that Pip felt it might be heard in the next room. The discouraging call proved unnerving. "I have a week left until I return home and take the boards. The position offered was not just as a clinic physician treating respiratory diseases, but a position having administrative power, which I hope to use to help improve working conditions," Pip mumbled.

However, judging from the call, he knew it may not include Valerie. He would be alone. Alone, like old doctor Willis.

"If I return, I'd have a golden opportunity to join John in the prestigious group on Harley Street. The dream of most young physicians starting out. That choice would include Valerie, bred for the job of a Harley Street physician's wife living in the city she loves. Our lives would be exciting, and rich," Pip said to himself.

After weighing both options, he knew what had to be done and made a choice.

CHAPTER 41: 1972-1973 HARLEY STREET

Pip, knowing well the requirements stipulated by Lord Perkins, accepted the position with the Wellesley Group on Harley Street. He convinced himself that patients, rich or poor, suffer from respiratory issues. He would help them recover using his expert knowledge, regardless of their background.

Before he left the clinic in South Wales, he thanked Dr. Willis for recommending him for the position. He explained his frustration of wanting the job versus his love of Valerie. He knew he could not have both and did not want to end it with Valerie.

Dr. Willis understood and convinced him that marriage was the better choice.

After working a few months at the Harley Street practice, Pip realized that it opened golden opportunities beyond his imagination...social standing, orchestra seats at the Royal Opera House, prime seats at football and rugby matches plus other amenities. Besides occupying the spacious office next to his best friend John, privileges granted him access to the best hospitals.

Uncle Stephen presented the young physician with one of the Juniper's newest models and carte blanch for two tailor made suits and appropriate shoes. "Stephen, your generosity overwhelms me. I can't accept gifts like this."

"Yes you can. Consider them an overdue endowment for you and my sister as well. No arguments."

Pip's protests fell on deaf ears and he modestly accepted the gracious gifts. Next, he needed a decent flat. Pip struggled to live within his starting income, but knew by saving enough, an affordable flat, close by, might save him a tiring commute. Upon reaching his goal, he planned to propose, since Valerie and her parents waited anxiously.

John alerted Pip about one of the senior physicians owning property near the practice. He promised to check for any available flats. Until one came along, he stayed with John, like old times.

Aside from examining patients, Pip made time to compile statistics on smoking and household occupants with respiratory issues. *Someday, when I have the time and adequate statistics, I'll write a paper and present it to my colleagues. Someday.*

After a year of hard work, everything worked out. The senior physician rented an available flat to Pip, a member of his staff, which made them both happy.

Before year's end, he proposed to Valerie keeping her and her over bearing parents fully engaged with lavish wedding preparations. The demand from work unintentionally diminished his passion to treat poor coal miners. Sadly, it slipped away into his subconscious.

CHAPTER 42: 1973 MARRIAGE

"Mummy, I can't wait to become Mrs. István Remke. I love him so much…he's all I could want in a man," Valerie proclaims, trying to repair a broken fingernail.

"Yes, Darling, in a couple of hours you'll become the wife of a Harley Street physician."

"He's just 'Pip' to me, and I would marry him even if he still wanted to treat coal miners."

"Valerie, dear, I could picture you washing his white lab coat caked with coal dust….treating men working in the dirty coal mines somewhere in a poor section of Wales or Pennsylvania where his father lived," says Lucinda sarcastically.

"Pip's heart is in the right place and my heart is with him. I love this man."

"I won't have to worry about you financially. Your trust will take care of you and your family for the rest of your lives. Dear Aunt Violet, God rest her soul, gave me sound advice. I really miss her."

"I know you do, Mummy," Valerie said, placing her hands on her mum's.

"Practically raised me on her own. When I told her I wanted to marry your father, she set up a special trust just for me. A year later, when she was convinced our marriage was solid; your father was given a generous share. In spite of the fact, he made wise decisions in his investments, Aunt Violet would request an accounting each quarter. Thank goodness it all worked out."

"Enough of this financial talk," Valerie said, "I am ecstatic and I know you are happy for me. Convince Daddy to be happy for me too."

"Silly, we BOTH are happy," her mum stated, her eyes smiling as she looked at her daughter.

CHAPTER 43: 1974 HEARTBREAK

"I can't go on. It should never have happened! So young...she was too damn young. Fate is bloody unfair!" Pip cried, as he sat in his office with John.

"Pip, old chap, try to pull yourself together. There was nothing you could do to prevent it. Valerie was a healthy young woman. She received the best of care," John said, trying to console his friend. "You're back at work just one week after the funeral. You need time to grieve...put your things in order."

Ignoring John's suggestion, Pip, muttered, "In spite of it all, we lost her. Her obstetrician reassured me there was no indication of an embolism...she went into cardiac arrest. Her prolonged labor caused our son's fetal distress. My son...poor innocent baby. I lost both, John, both of them before I could give them all I hoped to give."

Pacing about the office, John was about to say something, but Pip continued, "She should have had a C-section," Pip cried. "Why didn't I insist? Valerie was determined to have natural childbirth. She would have preferred to give birth at home. It was me who convinced her to come to the medical center...finest team of physicians and staff," he continued to sob.

"Pip, ole chap," John chimes in, "you can't blame yourself. You know that."

"So many plans for our future. She loved being part of the physicians' wives group and donating time to help the less fortunate. She really enjoyed helping people. So kind and giving. Bloody damn. Should have used birth control. I was an idiot…caught up in a moment of passion," Pip said, and then gazed out the office window at the gray day as he remembered their last conversation.

"Darling, sorry I woke you. I tried to be quiet." Valerie had said.

"No worry, Sweet. What's the problem?" Pip asked.

"I'm feeling dreadful. The sheer bulkiness of my body, puffy ankles, the weight gain. Maybe something is wrong."

"Let me lift the covers…check your ankles. I understand the last month of a woman's pregnancy can be uncomfortable. It's going to pass after the baby arrives. I'm more concerned about your high blood pressure though. I'll check it again," Pip said, doing so. "You must despise me for putting you in this state."

"Maybe a little, sometimes," she jests. "Though earlier than we planned, I wanted this baby so much," she smiled.

Sitting next to her on her bed, stroking her arm, "I'm cancelling my patients today. You need me more than they do."

"Don't be silly. I'll be fine. Only one more month, a short time. We'll get through it. Please go. Don't worry about me," she said cupping and squeezing his hand.

"On the condition you stay in bed. Nurse will be here shortly. Have her prop up your feet. No salt, understand?"

"*Yes, Doctor Remke*. What time will you be home?"

Looking over his pocket calendar, " Hmmm…. my last patient cancelled. I'll be right back home by five."

"I'll be here waiting. Cook can serve our dinner up here, in our bedroom."

"Smashing idea, Love."

"Cheers, Darling. I love you."

"Love you too," he said, kissing her before he left.

Blankly staring across the room, an inconsolable Pip continued, "John, that was the last time I heard her voice. Why didn't I stay home? She needed me. The secretary could have rescheduled the rest of my appointments. It's my fault."

Pouring Pip some whiskey, "Drink this, it might help calm you."

Pip gratefully accepts his friend's offer, consuming the fiery liquid in one generous gulp.

"How could you have foreseen this? Sure, her symptoms were atypical, but not extreme," John said, pouring his friend a second glass.

"Damn it. She died, John! My sweet Valerie and my baby died!" Pip muttered, before downing the second glass of whiskey wondering if the emptiness in his heart would ever find peace.

CHAPTER 44: 1974 NEW START, COAL MINERS' HOSPITAL

On top of a bleak looking hill, surrounded by random piles of coal waste and patches of green/brown grass, sits Coal Miner's Hospital, a one hundred bed facility in Coalville, Pennsylvania. Its location allows observation of the workers' activity over the mountain on the other side of the highway. The mountain, itself contains the deeply cut mines.

With the help of generous benefactors, the small hospital first served the mining community and their families. Although the number of coal mines declined over numerous years, they remained productive. Mining management companies brought in new technology, allowing the hospital to remain solvent.

"Another mining accident, Doctor. I've alerted the emergency crew."

"How many this time?"

"Hard to tell. A dozen or more?"

"Why in God's name do they keep the bloody mine open? The equipment violates so many regulations, and they already stripped away the best coal. Besides, people don't heat their homes with coal anymore."

"We both agree, Doctor, not in this part of the woods, however they still pull low grade coal out of the ground. The greedy capitalist owns a trucking company, so he can transport it to other parts of the world. Besides, the local men need work. Very little employment here, unless you own a business or practice as a doctor, dentist or lawyer."

Replacing his eyeglasses, covering weary green eyes, the physician responds, "I've heard it before, Nurse, Miss…"

Leaning closer to the new physician, she answers with a wink, "Miss Kelly, Erin Kelly. I am the evening supervisor for the hospital."

"Thank you, Miss Kelly, you seem well versed with the mining industry in this area."

Blushing, "I was born in this hospital and raised in the area."

"Then, I will certainly consider you a good resource. Can you elaborate on the safety conditions?"

Miss Kelly reveals the ugly truth, "The conditions never improve for the employees. The mine owners have a moral obligation to spend their money and build in more safety standards. State inspectors examine the mine, find violations and fine the company. In reality, they pay them off and do not improve working conditions."

"How do they expect to prevent accidents and lung disorders if they don't enforce standards?"

"Doctor, we all know it's a problem. Hopefully the new equipment will help efficiency and protect the miners."

Trying to soften his tone, "I can see them placing men on stretchers. Have the units been alerted for their arrival?"

Reassuringly Erin replies, "Of course, Doctor. They respond like clockwork."

"It's going to be another long night, I can see," the physician says wearily.

"I'll have the aide make us some coffee. OK?"

The familiar scent of Miss Kelly's floral cologne reminded him of late wife. He used to tease her that she smelled delicious, like a spring bouquet. *He figured the memory would always remain, but when does the bloody guilt go away?*

"Here Doctor, the hot coffee will keep you going. Milk and sugar?"

"Yes, please. Two sugars."

The nurse impressed him with her efficiency amidst the chaotic episode. Her actions produced a calming effect, in spite of the dangerous circumstances. He smiled, "It's the first time I noticed the extent of her talents."

While the emergency team triages the worst patients, The physician starts the grim task of examining the injured.

While he tends to their wounds, no one notices how time and grief slowly sprinkled his blonde hair with strands of silver.

"Why in the devil did I ever allow myself to accept this assignment to Coalville, Pennsylvania?" he whispers.

With little time to ponder, he sets to his task of assessing conditions of the men. After working through the night, he affixes his signature to the last medical record, István Remke, M.D. Respiratory Specialist.

Things did not look good for any of them. Not as long as conditions in the mines remain the same.

CHAPTER 45: 1974 A DAY IN THE LIFE

The telephone buzzed over and over, waking Pip after only one cherished hour of sleep. After two cups of coffee and a blueberry muffin, he was off to work.

While starting morning rounds on the units, familiar faces appear. The miners, or "repeat offenders" as they're called, return with their breathing issues. The travesty of it all - the mines, coal dust, smoking, poor lifestyle and splintered family units, add up to an unhealthy and stressful lifestyle.

"C'mon, old chap, deep breath, you can do it. Try to expand those lungs," Pip says to a middle-aged miner sitting before him.

"Aw Doc, it hurts like hell. Can't breathe, deep, I mean. Coughing won't stop. My old lady says she'll divorce me if she can't get some sleep....says I keep her up all night, hackin an coughin."

"Did you take your medicine? The red stuff I gave you?"

"When I remember."

"Mr. Shaminski, it's important. The medicine, deep breathing and drinking fluid, excluding beer, all important to the first steps to regaining your health."

"Doc, as soon as my son finishes college, I'm retiring...if I live that long."

"At least you have something to live for. That's a worthy goal. Keep that in mind next time you reach for a beer," Pip reminds him.

CHAPTER 46: 1974 CHANCE MEETING

On a well earned day off, Pip planned a swim in the Bungalow, Tamaqua's community pool. Although physicians and folks in higher standing were local country club members; he chose not to join that league. He did not play golf, tennis or cards. Free time was at a premium, so a few laps in the pool for exercise and an hour or two with a good book more than sufficed.

Keeping in step with his lean years at Oxford, Pip packed a sandwich and a bottle of soda water to wash it down. Finding an isolated, shady spot, he hunkered down to read the book that had been gathering dust on his nightstand.

"Bliminy," he murmured out loud, "Of all professions, I chose medicine, not only medicine, but caring for the poor in a deprived mining community. What was I thinking? Most of my Oxford colleagues are successful, working in their families' law firms, managing their businesses or physicians on Harley Street. Here I am, trying to save the lives of those already damned," Pip lamented.

"Dr. Remke, excuse me, but are you OK? You seem preoccupied!"

Struggling to rise, blubbering, "Of course, just daydreaming. Reasoning with myself. Miss Kelly, I hardly recognized you without your uniform. Join me?"

"Thank you, I wouldn't mind. It's the first time I could get away…nice to get out of uniform and have someone to talk to for a change."

"I assume you have a place nearby, close to Coal Miners' Hospital."

"Yes Dr. Remke. I live a mile away…in Lansburg, I was born there. I can tell from the way you speak, this is not your native territory," Miss Kelly said.

"Pip, please. I'm from London."

The red haired Miss Kelly sat down along side Pip and responds, "Please call me Erin, Pip. You're a long way from home. Do you miss it?"

"Definitely, but I've lived in so many places, I seem to adjust after a fashion."

"And what brought you to Coalville, Pennsylvania? I mean, the position at Coal Miners' Hospital. It was that tempting to cross the Atlantic?" she questioned, studying him.

Not wanting to readily open up his feelings to a stranger, Pip hedged his responses until he could sense Erin's sincerity.

Erin went on coaxing him to relax, "Are you finding it easy to adjust?"

"It's not my first time. Dad brought me to the States about ten years ago. My grandparents lived in New England Valley, near Tamaqua and raised my father there.

Gram and Grampa passed from natural causes, over the last few years. My father handled all the details of their funerals since I was in the middle of medical school. I visit their graves in Hometown when I can get away.

After they talk back and forth, Pip, began to feel more comfortable. Erin had a special gift of making people relaxed and showing she cared. Pip's eyes welled with tears when he told her about the recent personal tragedy in his life. "I cannot stop the guilt I feel for Valerie's death."

He poured out his feeling about the guilt he suffered for his wife's death. "It's my fault. I never should have left." Pip let his tears flow.

Erin reacted to his tears. She placed her arm around the sad man and held him. "Pip, it's okay to cry. You've suffered a great loss. Only time will lessen the pain."

"I'm sorry, but I can't stop."

"Please, no apologies. Tell me about your father and how he lives in England."

Pip recanted the story of his father's Air Force experience, meeting his mother and finding out about him.

"What possessed you to choose respiratory diseases for a specialty?" Erin asked.

"I had my first encounter with the veteran chaps. My father's friends, I met when I first traveled to the US. They worked in the mines and struggled with their breathing."

"You were perceptive, that's interesting and sensitive," Erin said.

"Then I met an old friend. He lived in South Wales. I was still a resident physician but after a short reconnection, he died."

Pip sobs, "He died in my arms during a mining accident."

Erin stroked his neck, and then gave him a reassuring hug. She changed the subject to a lighter note.

"I'll bet you're thirsty. How about I get us a soda from the refreshment stand? They don't have much choice, but a cold soda will quench our thirst."

"Splendid," Pip said relieved of the subject change.

"I see you brought a sandwich, I brought one too. I'm not a fan of their greasy hamburgers," Erin admitted.

They continued to dialogue between eating and gulps of cold soda. Before they realized it, the sun was starting to set.

"Where did the day go? I've been babbling on about my life and never asked you a question about yours," Pip apologized.

"Pay it no mind, my life is very ordinary compared to yours. I enjoyed our afternoon," Erin smiled.

"Erin, would you care to join me in a pint…I mean a drink?"

"I would love to," she smiled, placing a hand on his arm.

CHAPTER 47: 1974 ERIN KELLY

While traveling to her home in Lansburg, PA, Erin made a detour to the state store and picked up a half gallon of Gallo Chablis. After her arduous shift at the hospital, she elevated her tired legs and sipped a glass of the white liquid to decompress.

Her five years back in Lansburg were a major adjustment after her university education and working in the bustling city that she loved. The decision to accept the full scholarship at Columbia University was bitter sweet.

Her father, a coal miner from Ireland married Bridgett, his next door neighbor while growing up. They were in love with each other from childhood and wanted to marry as soon as their parents gave them their blessings.

When they heard about mining jobs in the US, Erin's father and mother made the decision to make the move. By the time Erin was born, her hard working parents already acquired a small home just a couple of miles away from the mines in Lansburg, Pennsylvania. As an only child, Erin stayed close to her parents. Her dear mother cooked tasty dishes and sewed most of her clothes.

Erin's father always came directly home from the mines, never stalling for a drink at the bar. His sense of humor and stories of Ireland entertained her for hours. "I remember when Dad came home, he would tease me and asked how many boys I kissed. Then he would look at my mom and ask her the same." Erin said to herself.

As much as she loved her parents, Erin could not imagine staying in Lansburg. The small town reeked of dusty air from the mines and lacked opportunities for younger people. As an honor student, who wanted to become a nurse, Erin's science teacher encouraged her to apply for a nursing scholarship at her alma mater, Columbia University. When the scholarship came through, it offered Erin her free education and ticket away from the coal mining area.

Some of her classmates were quite happy to marry local boys and find local jobs, but most men and women went off to college or joined the service to see the world and serve their country. A few stayed behind to work in nearby communities.

"Why don't you study closer to home?" her mother would plead, "You'll be so far away from us."

Her father's comment, using his favorite expression had been, "Sweet Baby Jesus, the city is dangerous and yer mom will be saying novenas every day."

"I know Daddy. It will be the first time that I've been on my own. I need to try at least." Erin would plead.

"Remember, Croi, if it doesn't work out, you come home. Your room will always be ready for you." her dad would add.

As guilty as she felt, Erin needed to spread her wings and move on.

Living on Columbia University's large campus in the city was an exciting experience in itself: The stimulating classes, American and international student population, distinguished professors completed her Cinderella-like existence away from the tiny town and coal mines. The prestigious scholarship covered a four year nursing curriculum that included classes at Columbia University and clinical nursing experience at Columbia Presbyterian Medical Center.

After her college graduation, Erin worked in the clinical areas until she passed her state boards. She transferred to the Emergency Department, which was full of excitement that kept her stimulated. During her employment, the hospital picked up half of her tuition allowing her to complete a master's degree at Columbia. In the midst of everything, she still found time to date and enjoy a romance with Max, an OB-GYN resident at the hospital.

Life was good. Erin was in love with the work she was doing and equally in love with New York City and the handsome resident, Max. She became an ardent Yankee fan, saw almost every new Broadway show, opening museum exhibits and four or five operas a year at the Met. With all of the perks, in which she indulged herself, her biggest thrill was to invite her parents for a trip and show off "her" city.

Her twice yearly NYC treat included a taxi ride from Lansburg to Tamaqua, where her parents would meet the bus to take them to Port Authority. They would hail a taxi taking them to her apartment at Cabrini Terrace at 900 West 190th street next to Fort Tryon Park.

Erin requested a couple of vacation days when they would visit. It always included a Broadway show, Radio City performance and sometimes, a Circle Line ride around Manhattan.

Her parents saw how much she thrived in the city, but her father never stopped asking, "Croi, do ya think ye'll ever come home to work?"

Squeezing his calloused hand, she replied gently, "I doubt it Daddy. I love it here." She would note his downtrodden head and eyes welling with tears, he would return her answer with a reassuring wink.

One day, her phone rang and an official sounding voice gave her the dreaded news. Her parents had been visiting friends who lived on a lonely country road. It was dark and their car swerved to miss a deer-hit a tree. Her mother sitting in the passenger seat died on impact. Her father had been in critical condition and rushed to Coal Miner's hospital in the next town.

Erin took an extended leave to manage her mother's funeral arrangements and care for her father in their home. His recovery had been slow for he had no will to live without his beloved Bridgett.

As time passed, Erin saw no alternative but to give notice and remain in the small town she hastened to leave a few years ago.

Max tried to be understanding, but ultimately, they parted. He saw no career advantage in Lansburg or future plans in her life. She carried on alone to care for her disheartened parent. As the days passed, she often thought of his nickname for her, Croi, meaning "My Heart" in Gaelic.

CHAPTER 48: 1974 BACK HOME, LANSBURG, PA

Her father lingered for six months after the accident. Erin cared for him in his own house as long as she could. Refusing any type of rehabilitation or help with mobility, he adamantly remained in bed. His lungs filled with fluid due to pneumonia. Realizing her own limitations and reneging on her promise to let him die in his own home, she had him admitted to Coal Miners' Hospital and cared for him there.

He eventually suffered a fatal stroke. Erin did her best to keep him alive, but having no more will to live, her father drifted off to be with his beloved Bridgett.

Erin faced the choice of moving back to New York or remaining in the small town she desperately wanted to leave. Pushing thirty, living in the community where one marries after high school or soon after, she faced the threat of being a lonely spinster.

Her parents, old fashioned as they were, did not trust the banks. While reorganizing the house, Erin discovered EE bonds and fifty dollar bills hidden in an old tin lunchbox she once used for school lunches. It was a tidy sum that would carry her until she decided what path to take for her future.

The house was paid off and the 1962 Plymouth was miraculously restored after the accident. The garage mechanics replaced parts and repainted the entire car so it looked like a new, slightly outdated vehicle.

"Finding a job and remaining in Lansburg, seems the more practical thing to do, until I find something better," said Erin to herself, "It's not the same without Mom and Dad, but their memories keep me going."

Her dilemma was answered when Coal Miners' Hospital was seeking an evening supervisor. Over qualified with her master's degree, it did not bother her. It was a job, close to home (her home for the time being) and her Columbia Presbyterian Emergency Department experience made her more than qualified for handling trauma faced by the coal mine disasters.

CHAPTER 49: 1974-1975 LIFE IN THE PA SMALL TOWN

Pip's day was no different than the other days: respiratory clinic, surgery (lung biopsies), respiratory testing and rounds. Within his six months at Coal Miners' Hospital, he was seeing progress with miners who followed the rehab programs: stop smoking, proper diet, exercise and psychiatric help when needed. He added a stress reduction clinic for affected vets who worked in the mines. For the first time as a practicing physician he felt accomplishment in his work.

The relationship with Erin started to blossom. Recovering from previous experiences, he with Valerie's death and Erin losing Max and her love affair with NYC, they found comfort in each other's company.

The first time he slept over in her home, it was unlike the awkward wedding night with Valerie. Each had faced a world of hard work and sadness of death. The awkward pressure of a first sexual encounter was removed, so Pip felt relaxed and could be himself.

Erin invited Pip home after their shift at the hospital. Since she had cooked the day before she offered him her Shepherd's Pie. "It's my mom's special," she said.

His eyes were fixed on the tiny waist, encircled by the apron sash as she pulled out the mouth watering casserole from the refrigerator.

"Here, let me help you," Pip insisted, popping the heavy casserole into the oven. Their eyes met as he took the food dish. A rush of exhilaration ran through his body as he brushed against her. Erin blushed.

"Uh...uh, smells good. It's been a long time since I've eaten a home-cooked meal." Pip tried to control his sexual urge reacting to the smell of the food and the attractive cook with the tiny waist.

"I think you'll enjoy the dish, most of my friends have. Mind getting out the wine glasses?"

Pip removes glasses from the cupboard. "These okay?"

"No, the Waterford...on the second shelf. I bought them for my parents. Two from my first paycheck. I added six more, a few at a time when I had spare money."

"They're beautiful," Pip replied, being careful not to mention that he and Valerie received several sets of Waterford crystal as wedding gifts.

"There's white wine or if you prefer red, I have a jug of hearty burgundy," she smiled and pulled out plates from the cupboard.

"Red will be fine," Pip said, watching her every move.

They enjoyed their meal between sips of wine, and frequent eye contact.

"Umm," Pip groaned.

Smiling, Erin asked, "How's my cooking?"

"Even better than it looked. The cook looks even better!"

"My mom would be proud...proud I cooked her specialty and it received rave reviews." Erin tilted her head, chuckling.

"The cook deserves a reward."

"A reward, and what might it be, *Sir*?" she questioned sarcastically.

"This." Pip arose from his chair and planted a kiss on Erin's cheek.

Erin welcomed the kiss but was totally unprepared for this gesture. They finished their meal, topping it off with more flirting and another glass of wine.

After dinner, they cleared off the table and put the food away. "I'll just rinse the dishes and wash them later. Against their protests, I bought my folks a portable dish washer. It saves time…and."

Her words were cut off as he moved closer. She could feel his closeness and warm breath on the back of her neck, "Erin, why are we stalling? We've worked together and spent most of our free time together. You have feelings towards me, am I right?"

Surprised, but relieved he made the first move, "Of, of course I do. Can't you tell?"

"I assumed you were interested, yet I just hadn't been sure until tonight. We've both been through great losses. I want to, but I'm afraid," she admitted.

"Afraid?"

"Afraid of being hurt. Rejected. Left behind. Your contract ends in six months. What's going to happen?"

"I have not planned that far ahead. The clinic is running well and the programs are working. If I must say, it's the most rewarding experience I've ever had."

"I see."

"I did not finish. Being with you has made it so beautiful. You bring beauty and excitement to my life."

Pulling her close, inhaling her cologne, he covered her neck with soft kisses. "Oh yes. That red hair drives me crazy." Holding her tightly, he felt his body reacting. "You exude self confidence. The way you handle the establishment and are caring and warm towards patients. That's sexy. It's been driving me crazy sometimes."

Erin closed her eyes, wanting him. "Let's go upstairs."

In her bedroom, the one she slept in as a child, two bodies came together as one, lusting for each other. After making love again and again, Erin stood up and walked away.

"Erin, Darling, why…why are you walking away from me?"

"Pip, I'm afraid."

"Afraid of what?"

"In six months you'll leave. Where will that leave me…us?" Erin reiterated.

"Six months is a long time. I care about you, and if the last hour of love making was any indication, you definitely care about me. If you don't, you have a silly way of showing it."

Laughing, "I care a lot, it is just difficult."

"Tell you what. Let's spend all of our free time together. *Out* of the hospital."

"Ok. Do you like to dance?"

"Yes. Of course. My dad taught me. It'll give me a chance to hold you close," Pip confessed.

"Is *that* what you want to do, Mr. Pip?" she blushes.

"Yes," he said, stepping closer.

They shared another passionate kiss and hugged good night before he drove away.

Erin slept soundly, still inhaling his scent, feeling things were going to be different this time.

The first time they had an entire day off together, they planned a picnic. Erin was in charge of the food and Pip contributed a six pack, one of the blankets courtesy of Coal Miners' Hospital and the transportation.

"Why won't you tell me where we're going?" Erin teased.

"Because I want to surprise you."

Pip arrived at Erin's home finding her, basket in hand, ready to go.

"Still not telling me?"

"Hold onto your knickers, woman, you'll see soon enough," Pip teased.

He drove through a rural area, past farm country until they came upon an isolated spot along side of a brook. He stopped, unloaded the car and they spread the blanket over the clumps of grass and forest remnants. "What do you think?"

"Perfect, how on earth did you find this spot? It's perfect," Erin smiled and gave him a big hug.

"Food, woman. Passion after. This man is hungry," Pip said.

Pretending to obey his orders, Erin saluted and placed containers of sliced ham sandwiches, home-made potato salad and coal slaw onto the blanket. A pitcher of freshly made iced tea with lemon helped to wash down the ample portions of food.

After removing the remains of their feast, Pip and Erin stretched out on the blanket.

"Passion time," dictated Pip, as he turned to kiss her softly, then deeply, "I don't want this to end, Darling, it's painful when I have to leave you. I wish I didn't have to."

"I know," Erin responded, "I feel it as well. I have a house...awfully big for just one person."

"Are you suggesting I move in with you?" Pip hedged.

"How would you feel about it?"

"I was going to suggest it, that is if you want to. Your neighbors will be tongue wagging for sure."

"I don't care. Let them talk. Their gossip can't hurt my folks anymore."

Pip hugged her tightly. They kissed passionately and for the last time, drove back to their respective homes.

CHAPTER 50: 1975 CHOICES

Pip's contract was coming to an end in another month. Erin and Pip made the most of working and living together in a small town, but it was time to consider their futures.

Settled temporarily in Erin's home in Lansburg, they relaxed in the big kitchen after their evening meal was finished.

"Wine, Darling?" Pip asked.

"Please. I want to prolong our rare time off together. You look troubled," she said.

Pouring two glasses of wine and handing one to Erin, Pip confessed, "Darling, I love you but it's not fair to ask you to marry me until we decide on our future. I love you and want us to be together but a long distance marriage is not fair to you or to me."

"I know, Pip, I love you too and will follow you, wherever you decide to go. As a nurse, I'd be able to find a job anywhere," she reassured him.

"I understand, however, Harley Street isn't for me anymore. London, the city, I loved. I've changed and it would just bring back old memories if I moved back," Pip stated.

"You mean, your former life with your wife, of course?" Erin asked.

"Not just Valerie, but her bloody family. Her father and mother's attitude. Even my old friends have changed. John, my friend who shared so much of my life, when we spoke, he seemed like a stranger. He does not understand why I love what I am doing."

"New York, I loved it, but one has to have lots of money to live there comfortably. Also, I have no one since my parents died," Erin pondered.

Pip responded, "I have Dad, but he just opened a new dance studio in London at up-scale Drury Lane and his girlfriend, Mary, moved in with him. At least, I know he will be just fine, no matter what we decide to do.

"I've already talked to some of my associates about professional openings. One opportunity that has everyone abuzz is Doctors Without Borders."

"Doctors Without Borders? Tell me about it," Erin asked.

"It's relatively new. A volunteer organization where they recruit physicians and nurses to treat the poor population in other countries."

"Hmmm. We'll never get rich working there, you know that," Erin tells him.

"I'm not worried about that. I'm more interested to help people who need medical care."

Raising her eyebrows and laughing softly, "Sounds like the right thing for both of us. When do you want to go?"

"One last item, needs an answer," Pip said, moving closer.

"Yes."

"It's better to travel to places like this as a married couple."

"Dr. Remke, what are you asking?" Erin said, all smiles.

Pip takes out a ring.

"C'mere, let me show you."

Erin gazing at the ring. "I love you."

"Prove it. Kiss me woman."

END

Epilogue

Pip and Erin entered a world, rich in adventure and challenge, through Doctors Without Borders. During a 5 year period, they had saved numerous lives while serving at TB clinics, tent cities and remote villages on several continents.

Their son was born in the most isolated of regions and raised among many foreign cultures and languages. Walter Remke III, aka Trip, a remarkable child, has flourished in spite of their primitive living. He had gained a deeper and wider perception of the world than most children.

When Erin discovers she is pregnant with her second, she experiences complications, due to uncontrollable hypertension. Pip contacts his friend John, who convinces them to return to England. Back in London, Erin is placed under the care of a high risk pregnancy specialist who oversees the birth of a healthy baby girl. They name her Ilona after Pip's deceased mother.

After Erin recovers, they visit Pip's father, Uncle Steven and old friends. Pip also stays in touch with medical associates to catch up on current events and professional opportunities.

Although Pip never expected to have any contact with Lord and Lady Perkins, he receives a call from Lady Perkins. She says some friends from the Harley Street medical community told her about their return. Lady Perkins is humble, asking Pip, Erin and the children to visit them at the estate.

A once arrogant Lord Perkins greets them. With unspoken words, an old and sad looking man, reaches out and clasps Pip's hand firmly. He is joined by Lady Perkins who hugs Pip and then Erin. She smiles while looking down at the children and reaches out to Trip, then to little Ilona. Lady Perkins holds Ilona close to her chest and while smoothing the child's hair, tears gently fall down M'Lady's face. In a choked voice, she said, "Would you consider being part of our family again? You, Erin and the children are all we have."

Glossary

Black Lung - a lung disease from inhaling coal dust. The lungs become black instead of pink. Medical term is pneumoconiosis.

Bliminy - vulgar interjection, holy mackerel.

Bloke - my friend or my fellow.

Bloody - adverb intensifier.

Boeing 707 - a mid-sized, long-range, narrow-body, four-engine jet airliner built by Boeing Commercial Airplanes from 1958 to 1979. Its name is commonly pronounced as "seven oh seven". Versions of the aircraft have a capacity from 140 to 219 passengers and a range of 2,500 to 5,750 nautical miles (4,630 to 10,650 km) (Wikipedia).

Bullocks - used figuratively in colloquial British English as a noun to mean 'nonsense', an expletive following a minor accident or misfortune.

Chap - guy or fellow.

Colliery - a coal mine and its connected buildings.

Croi - Gaelic word for 'my heart'.

Discotheque - a night club where dancing takes place, started in Berkley Square, London, early 1960s.

Doctors Without Borders - a group which sends physicians and other health workers to some of the most destitute and dangerous parts of the world and encourages them not only to care for people, but also to condemn the injustices they encounter. The 1999 Nobel Peace Prize was awarded to Doctors Without Borders (in French, Medicins Sans Frontieres).

Doctors Without Borders was formed in 1971 by a group of French physicians, most of whom had worked for the International Red Cross in Biafra in 1968 and 1970. According to the group, they aimed to overcome two shortcomings of international aid, "that it offers too little medical assistance and that aid agencies are overly reticent in the face of the many legal and administrative obstacles to the provision of effective humanitarian relief."

Double-Decker - refers to a double-decker bus. A bus that has both an upper and lower level where people can sit.

Flat - British term for apartment.

Harley Street - the street where the prestigious private doctors flourish.

Mushy Peas - large dried peas, cooked with marrow fat. Found in working-class cafes and pubs.

Pint - an Imperial pint is twenty ounces, equivalent to 'a beer' in the US.

Ploughman's Lunch - a favorite at pubs. A large piece of bread, an enormous slab of cheese, a big chunk of butter and a few sour pickled onions.

Swinging London - was a youth-driven cultural revolution that took place in London during the mid-to-late 1960s emphasizing modernity and fun-loving hedonism.

Trolley - British term for a bed on wheels for moving patients in hospital (US equivalent of stretcher).

Twist - twist or rope tobacco is made up of rope-like strands of tobacco that have been twisted together and cured in that position, afterwards being cut. Some types of twist may either be chewed or smoked in a tobacco pipe, and some are exclusive to one method or the other.

Wanker - a term that literally means 'one who wanks (masturbates)' but has since become a general insult. It is a pejorative term of English origin common in Britain and other parts of the English-speaking world (mainly commonwealth nations), including Ireland, Australia and New Zealand. Wikipedia.

Bibliography

BOOKS

Bortolotti, Dan. *Hope in Hell: Inside the World of Doctors Without Borders*. New York: Firefly Books Ltd., 2004.

British Women. *Life in the United Kingdom, a Guide for New Residents*. 3rd edition. Crown Copyright, 2013.

Dublin, Thomas, and Walter Licht. *Creating The Anthracite Region. The Face of Decline: The Pennsylvania Anthracite Region in the Twentieth Century*. Ithaca: Cornell UP, 2005.

Johnson, Mark. *Caribbean Volunteers at War*. England: Pen & Sword Books, 2014.

Schur, Norman W. *British English A to Z*. New York: Skyhorse Publishing, 2013.

INTERNET RESEARCH

"Aberfan disaster." *Wikipedia*. 28 March 2017. https://en.wikipedia.org/wiki/Aberfan_disaster. Accessed 03 April 2017.

"Black British." *Wikipedia*. 18 March 2017. https://en.wikipedia.org/wiki/Black_British. Accessed 19 March 2017.

"Black Lung Disease." *WebMD*. 18 February 2017. http://www.webmd.com/lung/tc/black-lung-disease-topic-overview#1. Accessed 03 April 2017.

Castells, Tom. "The evolution of the middle class." *BBC News Magazine*. 16 January 2014. http://www.bbc.com/news/magazine-25744526. Accessed 12 June 2017.

"Coal mining." *Wikipedia*. 05 July 2017. http://www.conservapedia.com/Coal mining. Accessed 10 July 2017.

"Coalworker's pneumoconiosis." *Wikipedia*. 09 September 2017. https://en.wikipedia.org/wiki/Coalworker%27s_pneumoconiosis. Accessed 21 September 2017.

"Doctors Without Borders." *MedicineNet.com*. 13 May 2016. http://www.medicinenet.com/script/main/art.asp?articlekey=10840. Accessed 19 September 2017.

Goldhill, Olivia. "Bright state school pupils less likely to get into Oxford" 05 February 2001. http://www.telegraph.co.uk/education/universityeducation/9062467/Bright-state-school-pupils-less-likely-to-get-into-Oxford.html. Accessed 20 June 2017.

"Hertford College, Oxford." *Wikipedia*. 24 March, 2017. https://en.wikipedia.org/wiki/Hertford College, Oxford. Accessed 26 March 2017.

"History of anthracite coal mining in Pennsylvania." *Wikipedia*. 26 June 2017. https://en.wikipedia.org/wiki/History of anthracite coal mining in Pennsylvania. Accessed 01 September 2017.

"History of Anthracite Coal Mining." *Mine Safety and Health Administration. United States Department of Labor*. Web. 20 April 2014. http://www.msha.gov/District/Dist_01/History/history.htm#.U1Y4_MfZipJ Accessed 20 September 2017.

Johnson, Mark. "The untold story of the RAF's black Second World War fliers over Europe." *The National Archives Description.* 11 June 2014 http://media.nationalarchives.gov.uk/index.php/untold-story-raf-black-second-world-war-fliers-europe/ Accessed 05 April 2017.

Marsden, Jennifer S. "An insider's view of the American and UK medical systems." 01 January 2006. https://www.researchgate.net/publication/7334491_An_insider%27s_view_of_the_American_and_UK_medical_systems. Accessed 27 March 2017.

Matlock, Sherman. "Doctors Without Borders medical term definition." *AZ Dictionary.* 20 September 2017. https://www.azdictionary.com/medical-dictionary/term-definition/Doctors%20Without%20Borders. Accessed 23 September 2017.

McLaughlin, Katie. "5 things women couldn't do in the 1960s." http://www.cnn.com/2014/08/07/living/sixties-women-5-things/index.html. *CNN.* 25 August 2014. Accessed 4 June 2017.

"Medical school in the United Kingdom." *Wikipedia.* 23 January 2017. https://en.wikipedia.org/wiki/Medical_school_in_the_United_Kingdom. Accessed 25 January, 2017.

"Oxford University Medical School." *Wikipedia.* 19 November 2016. https://www.asme.org.uk/oxford-university-medical-school.html. Accessed 24 March 2017.

"Social class in the United Kingdom." *Wikipedia.* 20 June 2017. https://en.wikipedia.org/wiki/Social class in the United Kingdom. Accessed 23 June 2017.

Watson, Kimberley. "The 1960s The Decade that Shook Britain." *Historic UK.* 2016. http://www.historic-uk.com/CultureUK/The-1960s-The-Decade-that-Shook-Britain/. Accessed 17 April 2017.

NEWSPAPERS, JOURNALS AND MAGAZINES

Goodwin, Daisy. "Cash for titles: The Billion-dollar ladies." *You Magazine, Mail On Sunday.* 16 August 2010. Web.

Light, Donald W. PhD. "Universal Health Care: Lessons from the British Experience." *Am J Public Health.* 2003 January, 93(1): 25–30. Print.

Loyd, Linda. "Newcomer revives coal mine near Tamaqua." *Headlines Network.* 06 May 2012. Print.

White, Bill. "Coal Cracker Remembers." *The Morning Call* . 27 January 2017. Print.

Zagofsky, Al. "Lehigh Anthracite resurrects LC&N's coal operations." *Times News.* 01 June 2013. Print.

SPECIAL THANKS TO FOLKS FROM INTERVIEWS, DISCUSSIONS OR CORRESPONDENCE

England and Oxford. Michael Forrester, author.

Ireland. Paul Kealy. Ireland historian and tour guide.

Pennsylvania coal mines. Bill White and Tamaqua, PA, Facebook Group friends.

Wales. Alan Jones, mining.